D0250622

# BROKEBACK MOUNTAIN

## STORY TO SCREENPLAY

Annie Proulx,
Larry McMurtry
and Diana Ossana

SCRIBNER
New York London Toronto Sydney

SCRIBNER
1230 Avenue of the Americas
New York, NY 10020

"Brokeback Mountain" copyright © 1997 by Dead Line, Ltd.
Screenplay, cover, interior artwork, photographs copyright © 2005 by Focus Features LLC.
Licensed by Universal Studios Licensing LLLP. All Rights Reserved.
"Adapting Brokeback Mountain" copyright © 2005 by Larry McMurtry
"Climbing Brokeback Mountain" copyright © 2005 by Diana Ossana
"Getting Movied" copyright © 2005 by Dead Line, Ltd.

Photographs by Kimberley French

First Scribner trade paperback edition 2005

SCRIBNER and design are trademarks of Macmillan Library Reference USA, Inc., used under license by Simon & Schuster, the publisher of this work.

For information about special discounts for bulk purchases, please contact Simon & Schuster Special Sales:
1-800-456-6798 or business@simonandschuster.com

DESIGNED BY ERICH HOBBING

Text set in Bembo

Manufactured in the United States of America

1 3 5 7 9 10 8 6 4 2

Library of Congress Cataloging-in-Publication Data is available

ISBN-13: 978-0-7432-9416-4
ISBN-10: 0-7432-9416-5

"Brokeback Mountain" was originally published in *The New Yorker*

# Contents

# BROKEBACK MOUNTAIN

## STORY TO SCREENPLAY

# Brokeback Mountain

*Ennis del Mar wakes before five, wind rocking the trailer, hissing in around the aluminum door and window frames. The shirts hanging on a nail shudder slightly in the draft. He gets up, scratching the grey wedge of belly and pubic hair, shuffles to the gas burner, pours leftover coffee in a chipped enamel pan; the flame swathes it in blue. He turns on the tap and urinates in the sink, pulls on his shirt and jeans, his worn boots, stamping the heels against the floor to get them full on. The wind booms down the curved length of the trailer and under its roaring passage he can hear the scratching of fine gravel and sand. It could be bad on the highway with the horse trailer. He has to be packed and away from the place that morning. Again the ranch is on the market and they've shipped out the last of the horses, paid everybody off the day before, the owner saying, "Give em to the real estate shark, I'm out a here," dropping the keys in Ennis's hand. He might have to stay with his married daughter until he picks up another job, yet he is suffused with a sense of pleasure because Jack Twist was in his dream.*

*The stale coffee is boiling up but he catches it before it goes over the side, pours it into a stained cup and blows on the black liquid, lets a panel of the dream slide forward. If he does not force his attention on it, it might stoke the day, rewarm that old, cold time on the mountain when they owned the world and nothing seemed wrong. The wind strikes the trailer like a load of dirt coming off a dump truck, eases, dies, leaves a temporary silence.*

They were raised on small, poor ranches in opposite corners of the state, Jack Twist in Lightning Flat up on the Montana border, Ennis del Mar from around Sage, near the Utah line, both high school dropout country boys with no prospects, brought up to hard work and privation, both rough-mannered, rough-spoken, inured to the stoic life. Ennis, reared by his older brother and sister after their parents drove off the only curve on Dead Horse Road leaving them twenty-four dollars in cash and a two-mortgage ranch, applied at age fourteen for a hardship license that let him make the hour-long trip from the ranch to the high school. The pickup was old, no heater, one windshield wiper and bad tires; when the transmission went there was no money to fix it. He had wanted to be a sophomore, felt the word carried a kind of distinction, but the truck broke down short of it, pitching him directly into ranch work.

In 1963 when he met Jack Twist, Ennis was engaged to Alma Beers. Both Jack and Ennis claimed to be saving money for a small spread; in Ennis's case that meant a tobacco can with two five-dollar bills inside. That spring, hungry for any job, each had signed up with Farm and Ranch Employment—they came together on paper as herder and camp tender for the same sheep operation north of Signal. The summer range lay above the tree line on Forest Service land on Brokeback Mountain. It would be Jack Twist's second summer on the mountain, Ennis's first. Neither of them was twenty.

They shook hands in the choky little trailer office in front of a table littered with scribbled papers, a Bakelite ashtray brimming with stubs. The venetian blinds hung askew and admitted a triangle of white light, the shadow of the foreman's hand moving into it. Joe Aguirre, wavy hair the color of cigarette ash and parted down the middle, gave them his point of view.

"Forest Service got designated campsites on the allotments. Them camps can be a couple a miles from where we pasture the sheep. Bad predator loss, nobody near lookin after em at night. What I want, camp tender in the main camp where the Forest Service says, but the HERDER"—pointing at Jack with a chop of his hand—"pitch a pup tent on the q.t. with the sheep, out a sight, and he's goin a SLEEP there. Eat supper, breakfast in camp, but SLEEP WITH THE SHEEP, hunderd percent, NO FIRE, don't leave NO SIGN. Roll up that tent every mornin case Forest Service snoops around. Got the dogs, your .30-30, sleep there. Last summer had goddamn near twenty-five percent loss. I don't want that again. YOU," he said to Ennis, taking in the ragged hair, the big nicked hands, the jeans torn, button-gaping shirt, "Fridays twelve noon be down at the bridge with your next week list and mules. Somebody with supplies'll be there in a pickup." He didn't ask if Ennis had a watch but took a cheap round ticker on a braided cord from a box on a high shelf, wound and set it, tossed it to him as if he weren't worth the reach. "TOMORROW MORNIN we'll truck you up the jump-off." Pair of deuces going nowhere.

They found a bar and drank beer through the afternoon, Jack telling Ennis about a lightning storm on the mountain the year before that killed forty-two sheep, the peculiar stink of them and the way they bloated, the need for plenty of whiskey up there. He had shot an eagle, he said, turned his head to show the tail feather in his hatband. At first glance Jack seemed fair enough with his curly hair and quick laugh, but for a small man he carried some weight in the haunch and his smile disclosed buckteeth, not pronounced enough to let him eat popcorn out of the neck of a jug, but noticeable. He was infatuated with the rodeo life and fastened his belt with a minor bull-riding buckle, but his boots were worn to the quick, holed beyond repair and he was crazy to be somewhere, anywhere else than Lightning Flat.

Ennis, high-arched nose and narrow face, was scruffy and a little cave-chested, balanced a small torso on long, caliper legs, possessed a muscular and supple body made for the horse and for fighting. His reflexes were uncommonly quick and he was farsighted enough to dislike reading anything except Hamley's saddle catalog.

The sheep trucks and horse trailers unloaded at the trailhead and a bandy-legged Basque showed Ennis how to pack the mules, two packs and a riding load on each animal ring-lashed with double diamonds and secured with half hitches, telling him, "Don't never order soup. Them boxes a soup are real bad to pack." Three puppies belonging to one of the blue heelers went in a pack basket, the runt inside Jack's coat, for he loved a little dog. Ennis picked out a big chestnut called Cigar Butt to ride, Jack a bay mare who turned out to have a low startle point. The string of spare horses included a mouse-colored grullo whose looks Ennis liked. Ennis and Jack, the dogs, horses and mules, a thousand ewes and their lambs flowed up the trail like dirty water through the timber and out above the tree line into the great flowery meadows and the coursing, endless wind.

They got the big tent up on the Forest Service's platform, the kitchen and grub boxes secured. Both slept in camp that first night, Jack already bitching about Joe Aguirre's sleep-with-the-sheep-and-no-fire order, though he saddled the bay mare in the dark morning without saying much. Dawn came glassy orange, stained from below by a gelatinous band of pale green. The sooty bulk of the mountain paled slowly until it was the same color as the smoke from Ennis's breakfast fire. The cold air sweetened, banded pebbles and crumbs of soil cast sudden pencil-long shadows and the rearing lodgepole pines below them massed in slabs of somber malachite.

During the day Ennis looked across a great gulf and sometimes saw Jack, a small dot moving across a high meadow as an insect moves across a tablecloth; Jack, in his dark camp, saw Ennis as night fire, a red spark on the huge black mass of mountain.

Jack came lagging in late one afternoon, drank his two bottles of beer cooled in a wet sack on the shady side of the tent, ate two bowls of stew, four of Ennis's stone biscuits, a can of peaches, rolled a smoke, watched the sun drop.

"I'm commutin four hours a day," he said morosely. "Come in for breakfast, go back to the sheep, evenin get em bedded down, come in for supper, go back to the sheep, spend half the night jumpin up and checkin for coyotes. By rights I should be spendin the night here. Aguirre got no right a make me do this."

"You want a switch?" said Ennis. "I wouldn't mind herdin. I wouldn't mind sleepin out there."

"That ain't the point. Point is, we both should be in this camp. And that goddamn pup tent smells like cat piss or worse."

"Wouldn't mind bein out there."

"Tell you what, you got a get up a dozen times in the night out there over them coyotes. Happy to switch but give you warnin I can't cook worth a shit. Pretty good with a can opener."

"Can't be no worse than me, then. Sure, I wouldn't mind a do it."

They fended off the night for an hour with the yellow kerosene lamp and around ten Ennis rode Cigar Butt, a good night horse, through the glimmering frost back to the sheep, carrying leftover biscuits, a jar of jam and a jar of coffee with him for the next day saying he'd save a trip, stay out until supper.

"Shot a coyote just first light," he told Jack the next evening, sloshing his face with hot water, lathering up soap and hoping his razor had some cut left in it, while Jack peeled potatoes. "Big son of a bitch. Balls on him size a apples. I bet he'd took a few lambs. Looked like he could a eat a camel. You want some a this hot water? There's plenty."

"It's all yours."

"Well, I'm goin a warsh everthing I can reach," he said, pulling off his boots and jeans (no drawers, no socks, Jack noticed), slopping the green washcloth around until the fire spat.

They had a high-time supper by the fire, a can of beans each, fried potatoes and a quart of whiskey on shares, sat with their backs against a log, boot soles and copper jeans rivets hot, swapping the bottle while the lavender sky emptied of color and the chill air drained down, drinking, smoking cigarettes, getting up every now and then to piss, firelight throwing a sparkle in the arched stream, tossing sticks on the fire to keep the talk going, talking horses and rodeo, roughstock events, wrecks and injuries sustained, the submarine *Thresher* lost two months earlier with all hands and how it must have been in the last doomed minutes, dogs each had owned and known, the draft, Jack's home ranch where his father and mother held on, Ennis's family place folded years ago after his folks died, the older brother in Signal and a married sister in Casper. Jack said his father had been a pretty well known bullrider years back but kept his secrets to himself, never gave Jack a word of advice, never came once to see Jack ride, though he had put him on the woolies when he was a little kid. Ennis said the kind of riding that interested him lasted longer than eight seconds and had some point to it. Money's a good point, said Jack, and Ennis had to agree. They were respectful of each other's opinions, each glad to have a companion where none had been expected. Ennis, riding against the wind back to the sheep in the treacherous, drunken light, thought he'd never had such a good time, felt he could paw the white out of the moon.

The summer went on and they moved the herd to new pasture, shifted the camp; the distance between the sheep and the new camp was greater and the night ride longer. Ennis rode easy, sleeping with his eyes open, but the hours he was away from the sheep stretched out and out. Jack pulled a squalling burr out of the harmonica, flattened a little from a fall off the skittish bay mare, and Ennis had a good raspy voice; a few nights they mangled their way through some songs. Ennis knew the salty words to "Strawberry Roan." Jack tried a Carl Perkins song, bawling "what I say-ay-ay," but he favored a sad hymn, "Water-Walking Jesus," learned from his mother who believed in the Pentecost, that he sang at dirge slowness, setting off distant coyote yips.

"Too late to go out to them damn sheep," said Ennis, dizzy drunk on all fours one cold hour when the moon had notched past two. The meadow stones glowed white-green and a flinty wind worked over the meadow, scraped the fire low, then ruffled it into yellow silk sashes. "Got you a extra blanket I'll roll up out here and grab forty winks, ride out at first light."

"Freeze your ass off when that fire dies down. Better off sleepin in the tent."

"Doubt I'll feel nothin." But he staggered under canvas, pulled his boots off, snored on the ground cloth for a while, woke Jack with the clacking of his jaw.

"Jesus Christ, quit hammerin and get over here. Bedroll's big enough," said Jack in an irritable sleep-clogged voice. It was big enough, warm enough, and in a little while they deepened their intimacy considerably. Ennis ran full-throttle on all roads whether fence mending or money spending, and he wanted none of it when Jack seized his left hand and brought it to his erect cock. Ennis jerked his hand away as though he'd touched fire, got to his knees, unbuckled his belt, shoved his pants down, hauled Jack onto all fours and, with the help of the clear slick and a little spit, entered him, nothing he'd done before but no instruction manual needed. They went at it in silence except for a few sharp intakes of breath and Jack's choked "gun's goin *off,*" then out, down, and asleep.

Ennis woke in red dawn with his pants around his knees, a top-grade headache, and Jack butted against him; without saying anything about it both knew how it would go for the rest of the summer, sheep be damned.

As it did go. They never talked about the sex, let it happen, at first only in the tent at night, then in the full daylight with the hot sun striking down, and at evening in the fire glow, quick, rough, laughing and snorting, no lack of noises, but saying not a goddamn word except once Ennis said, "I'm not no queer," and Jack jumped in with "Me neither. A one-shot thing. Nobody's business but ours." There were only the two of them on the mountain flying in the euphoric, bitter air, looking down on the hawk's back and the crawling lights of vehicles on the plain below, suspended above ordinary affairs and distant from tame ranch dogs barking in the dark hours. They believed themselves invisible, not knowing Joe Aguirre had watched them through his 10x42 binoculars for ten minutes one day, waiting until they'd buttoned up their jeans, waiting until Ennis rode back to the sheep, before bringing up the message that Jack's people had sent word that his uncle Harold was in the hospital with pneumonia and expected not to make it. Though he did, and Aguirre came up again to say so, fixing Jack with his bold stare, not bothering to dismount.

In August Ennis spent the whole night with Jack in the main camp and in a blowy hailstorm the sheep took off west and got among a herd in another allotment. There was a damn miserable time for five days, Ennis and a Chilean herder with no English trying to sort them out, the task almost impossible as the paint brands were worn and faint at this late season. Even when the numbers were right Ennis knew the sheep were mixed. In a disquieting way everything seemed mixed.

The first snow came early, on August thirteenth, piling up a foot, but was followed by a quick melt. The next week Joe Aguirre sent word to bring them down—another, bigger storm was moving in from the Pacific—and they packed in the game and moved off the mountain with the sheep, stones rolling at their heels, purple cloud crowding in from the west and the metal smell of coming snow pressing them on. The mountain boiled with demonic energy, glazed with flickering broken-cloud light, the wind combed the grass and drew from the damaged krummholz and slit rock a bestial drone. As they descended the slope Ennis felt he was in a slow-motion, but headlong, irreversible fall.

Joe Aguirre paid them, said little. He had looked at the milling sheep with a sour expression, said, "Some a these never went up there with you." The count was not what he'd hoped for either. Ranch stiffs never did much of a job.

"You goin a do this next summer?" said Jack to Ennis in the street, one leg already up in his green pickup. The wind was gusting hard and cold.

"Maybe not." A dust plume rose and hazed the air with fine grit and he squinted against it. "Like I said, Alma and me's gettin married in December. Try to get somethin on a ranch. You?" He looked away from Jack's jaw, bruised blue from the hard punch Ennis had thrown him on the last day.

"If nothin better comes along. Thought some about going back up to my daddy's place, give him a hand over the winter, then maybe head out for Texas in the spring. If the draft don't get me."

"Well, see you around, I guess." The wind tumbled an empty feed bag down the street until it fetched up under his truck.

"Right," said Jack, and they shook hands, hit each other on the shoulder, then there was forty feet of distance between them and nothing to do but drive away in opposite directions. Within a mile Ennis felt like someone was pulling his guts out hand over hand a yard at a time. He stopped at the side of the road and, in the whirling new snow, tried to puke but nothing came up. He felt about as bad as he ever had and it took a long time for the feeling to wear off.

In December Ennis married Alma Beers and had her pregnant by mid-January. He picked up a few short-lived ranch jobs, then settled in as a wrangler on the old Elwood Hi-Top place north of Lost Cabin in Washakie County. He was still working there in September when Alma Jr., as he called his daughter, was born and their bedroom was full of the smell of old blood and milk and baby shit, and the sounds were of squalling and sucking and Alma's sleepy groans, all reassuring of fecundity and life's continuance to one who worked with livestock.

When the Hi-Top folded they moved to a small apartment in Riverton up over a laundry. Ennis got on the highway crew, tolerating it but working weekends at the Rafter B in exchange for keeping his horses out there. The second girl was born and Alma wanted to stay in town near the clinic because the child had an asthmatic wheeze.

"Ennis, please, no more damn lonesome ranches for us," she said, sitting on his lap, wrapping her thin, freckled arms around him. "Let's get a place here in town?"

"I guess," said Ennis, slipping his hand up her blouse sleeve and stirring the silky armpit hair, then easing her down, fingers moving up her ribs to the jelly breast, over the round belly and knee and up into the wet gap all the way to the north pole or the equator depending which way you thought you were sailing, working at it until she shuddered and bucked against his hand and he rolled her over, did quickly what she hated. They stayed in the little apartment which he favored because it could be left at any time.

* * *

The fourth summer since Brokeback Mountain came on and in June Ennis had a general delivery letter from Jack Twist, the first sign of life in all that time.

*Friend this letter is a long time over due. Hope you get it. Heard you was in Riverton. Im coming thru on the 24th, thought Id stop and buy you a beer. Drop me a line if you can, say if your there.*

The return address was Childress, Texas. Ennis wrote back, *you bet,* gave the Riverton address.

The day was hot and clear in the morning, but by noon the clouds had pushed up out of the west rolling a little sultry air before them. Ennis, wearing his best shirt, white with wide black stripes, didn't know what time Jack would get there and so had taken the day off, paced back and forth, looking down into a street pale with dust. Alma was saying something about taking his friend to the Knife & Fork for supper instead of cooking it was so hot, if they could get a baby-sitter, but Ennis said more likely he'd just go out with Jack and get drunk. Jack was not a restaurant type, he said, thinking of the dirty spoons sticking out of the cans of cold beans balanced on the log.

Late in the afternoon, thunder growling, that same old green pickup rolled in and he saw Jack get out of the truck, beat-up Resistol tilted back. A hot jolt scalded Ennis and he was out on the landing pulling the door closed behind him. Jack took the stairs two and two. They seized each other by the shoulders, hugged mightily, squeezing the breath out of each other, saying, son of a bitch, son of a bitch, then, and easily as the right key turns the lock tumblers, their mouths came together, and hard, Jack's big teeth bringing blood, his hat falling to the floor, stubble rasping, wet saliva welling, and the door opening and Alma looking out for a few seconds at Ennis's straining shoulders and shutting the door again and still they clinched, pressing chest and groin and thigh and leg together, treading on each other's toes until they pulled apart to breathe and Ennis, not big on endearments, said what he said to his horses and daughters, little darlin.

The door opened again a few inches and Alma stood in the narrow light.

What could he say? "Alma, this is Jack Twist, Jack, my wife Alma." His chest was heaving. He could smell Jack—the intensely familiar odor of cigarettes, musky sweat and a faint sweetness like grass, and with it the rushing cold of the mountain. "Alma," he said, "Jack and me ain't seen each other in four years." As if it were a reason. He was glad the light was dim on the landing but did not turn away from her.

"Sure enough," said Alma in a low voice. She had seen what she had seen. Behind her in the room lightning lit the window like a white sheet waving and the baby cried.

"You got a kid?" said Jack. His shaking hand grazed Ennis's hand, electrical current snapped between them.

"Two little girls," Ennis said. "Alma Jr. and Francine. Love them to pieces." Alma's mouth twitched.

"I got a boy," said Jack. "Eight months old. Tell you what, I married a cute little old Texas girl down in Childress—Lureen." From the vibration of the floorboard on which they both stood Ennis could feel how hard Jack was shaking.

"Alma," he said. "Jack and me is goin out and get a drink. Might not get back tonight, we get drinkin and talkin."

"Sure enough," Alma said, taking a dollar bill from her pocket. Ennis guessed she was going to ask him to get her a pack of cigarettes, bring him back sooner.

"Please to meet you," said Jack, trembling like a run-out horse.

"Ennis—" said Alma in her misery voice, but that didn't slow him down on the stairs and he called back, "Alma, you want smokes there's some in the pocket a my blue shirt in the bedroom."

They went off in Jack's truck, bought a bottle of whiskey and within twenty minutes were in the Motel Siesta jouncing a bed. A few handfuls of hail rattled against the window followed by rain and slippery wind banging the unsecured door of the next room then and through the night.

* * *

The room stank of semen and smoke and sweat and whiskey, of old carpet and sour hay, saddle leather, shit and cheap soap. Ennis lay spread-eagled, spent and wet, breathing deep, still half tumescent, Jack blowing forceful cigarette clouds like whale spouts, and Jack said, "Christ, it got a be all that time a yours ahorseback makes it so goddamn good. We got to talk about this. Swear to god I didn't know we was goin a get into this again—yeah, I did. Why I'm here. I fuckin knew it. Redlined all the way, couldn't get here fast enough."

"I didn't know where in the *hell* you was," said Ennis. "Four years. I about give up on you. I figured you was sore about that punch."

"Friend," said Jack, "I was in Texas rodeoin. How I met Lureen. Look over on that chair."

On the back of the soiled orange chair he saw the shine of a buckle. "Bullridin?"

"Yeah. I made three fuckin thousand dollars that year. Fuckin starved. Had to borrow everthing but a toothbrush from other guys. Drove grooves across Texas. Half the time under that cunt truck fixin it. Anyway, I didn't never think about losin. Lureen? There's some serious money there. Her old man's got it. Got this farm machinery business. Course he don't let her have none a the money, and he hates my fuckin guts, so it's a hard go now but one a these days—"

"Well, you're goin a go where you look. Army didn't get you?" The thunder sounded far to the east, moving from them in its red wreaths of light.

"They can't get no use out a me. Got some crushed vertebrates. And a stress fracture, the arm bone here, you know how bullridin you're always leverin it off your thigh?—she gives a little ever time you do it. Even if you tape it good you break it a little goddamn bit at a time. Tell you what, hurts like a bitch afterwards. Had a busted leg. Busted in three places. Come off the bull and it was a big bull with a lot a drop, he got rid a me in about three flat and he come after me and he was sure faster. Lucky enough. Friend a mine got his oil checked with a horn dipstick and that was all she wrote. Bunch a other things, fuckin busted ribs, sprains and pains, torn ligaments. See, it ain't like it was in my daddy's time. It's guys with money go to college, trained athaletes. You got a have some money to rodeo now. Lureen's old man wouldn't give me a dime if I dropped it, except one way. And I know enough about the game now so I see that I ain't never goin a be on the bubble. Other reasons. I'm gettin out while I still can walk."

Ennis pulled Jack's hand to his mouth, took a hit from the cigarette, exhaled. "Sure as hell seem in one piece to me. You know, I was sittin up here all that time tryin to figure out if I was—? I know I ain't. I mean here we both got wives and kids, right? I like doin it with women, yeah, but Jesus H., ain't nothin like this. I never had no thoughts a doin it with another guy except I sure wrang it out a hunderd times thinkin about you. You do it with other guys? Jack?"

"Shit no," said Jack, who had been riding more than bulls, not rolling his own. "You know that. Old Brokeback got us good and it sure ain't over. We got a work out what the fuck we're goin a do now."

"That summer," said Ennis. "When we split up after we got paid out I had gut cramps so bad I pulled over and tried to puke, thought I ate somethin bad at that place in Dubois. Took me about a year a figure out it was that I shouldn't a let you out a my sights. Too late then by a long, long while."

"Friend," said Jack. "We got us a fuckin situation here. Got a figure out what to do."

"I doubt there's nothin now we can do," said Ennis. "What I'm sayin, Jack, I built a life up in them years. Love my little girls. Alma? It ain't her fault. You got your baby and wife, that place in Texas. You and me can't hardly be decent together if what happened back there"—he jerked his head in the direction of the apartment—"grabs on us like that. We do that in the wrong place we'll be dead. There's no reins on this one. It scares the piss out a me."

"Got to tell you, friend, maybe somebody seen us that summer. I was back there the next June, thinkin about goin back—I didn't, lit out for Texas instead—and Joe Aguirre's in the office and he says to me, he says, 'You boys found a way to make the time pass up there, didn't you,' and I give him a look but when I went out I seen he had a big-ass pair a binoculars hangin off his rearview." He neglected to add that the foreman had leaned back in his squeaky wooden tilt chair, said, Twist, you guys wasn't gettin paid to leave the dogs baby-sit the sheep while you stemmed the rose, and declined to rehire him. He went on, "Yeah, that little punch a yours surprised me. I never figured you to throw a dirty punch."

"I come up under my brother K.E., three years older'n me, slugged me silly ever day. Dad got tired a me come bawlin in the house and when I was about six he set me down and says, Ennis, you got a problem and you got a fix it or it's gonna be with you until you're ninety and K.E.'s ninety-three. Well, I says, he's bigger'n me. Dad says, you got a take him unawares, don't say nothin to him, make him feel some pain, get out fast and keep doin it until he takes the message. Nothin like hurtin somebody to make him hear good. So I did. I got him in the outhouse, jumped him on the stairs, come over to his pillow in the night while he was sleepin and pasted him damn good. Took about two days. Never had trouble with K.E. since. The lesson was, don't say nothin and get it over with quick." A telephone rang in the next room, rang on and on, stopped abruptly in mid-peal.

"You won't catch me again," said Jack. "Listen. I'm thinkin, tell you what, if you and me had a little ranch together, little cow and calf operation, your horses, it'd be some sweet life. Like I said, I'm gettin out a rodeo. I ain't no broke-dick rider but I don't got the bucks a ride out this slump I'm in and I don't got the bones a keep gettin wrecked. I got it figured, got this plan, Ennis, how we can do it, you and me. Lureen's old man, you bet he'd give me a bunch if I'd get lost. Already more or less said it—"

"Whoa, whoa, whoa. It ain't goin a be that way. We can't. I'm stuck with what I got, caught in my own loop. Can't get out of it. Jack, I don't want a be like them guys you see around sometimes. And I don't want a be dead. There was these two old guys ranched together down home, Earl and Rich—Dad would pass a remark when he seen them. They was a joke even though they was pretty tough old birds. I was what, nine years old and they found Earl dead in a irrigation ditch. They'd took a tire iron to him, spurred him up, drug him around by his dick until it pulled off, just bloody pulp. What the tire iron done looked like pieces a burned tomatoes all over him, nose tore down from skiddin on gravel."

"You seen that?"

"Dad made sure I seen it. Took me to see it. Me and K.E. Dad laughed about it. Hell, for all I know he done the job. If he was alive and was to put his head in that door right now you bet he'd go get his tire iron. Two guys livin together? No. All I can see is we get together once in a while way the hell out in the back a nowhere—"

"How much is once in a while?" said Jack. "Once in a while ever four fuckin years?"

"No," said Ennis, forbearing to ask whose fault that was. "I goddamn hate it that you're goin a drive away in the mornin and I'm goin back to work. But if you can't fix it you got a stand it," he said. "Shit. I been lookin at people on the street. This happen a other people? What the hell do they do?"

"It don't happen in Wyomin and if it does I don't know what they do, maybe go to Denver," said Jack, sitting up, turning away from him, "and I don't give a flyin fuck. Son of a bitch, Ennis, take a couple days off. Right now. Get us out a here. Throw your stuff in the back a my truck and let's get up in the mountains. Couple a days. Call Alma up and tell her you're goin. Come on, Ennis, you just shot my airplane out a the sky—give me somethin a go on. This ain't no little thing that's happenin here."

The hollow ringing began again in the next room, and as if he were answering it, Ennis picked up the phone on the bedside table, dialed his own number.

A slow corrosion worked between Ennis and Alma, no real trouble, just widening water. She was working at a grocery store clerk job, saw she'd always have to work to keep ahead of the bills on what Ennis made. Alma asked Ennis to use rubbers because she dreaded another pregnancy. He said no to that, said he would be happy to leave her alone if she didn't want any more of his kids. Under her breath she said, "I'd have em if you'd support em." And under that, thought, anyway, what you like to do don't make too many babies.

Her resentment opened out a little every year: the embrace she had glimpsed, Ennis's fishing trips once or twice a year with Jack Twist and never a vacation with her and the girls, his disinclination to step out and have any fun, his yearning for low-paid, long-houred ranch work, his propensity to roll to the wall and sleep as soon as he hit the bed, his failure to look for a decent permanent job with the county or the power company, put her in a long, slow dive and when Alma Jr. was nine and Francine seven she said, what am I doin hangin around with him, divorced Ennis and married the Riverton grocer.

Ennis went back to ranch work, hired on here and there, not getting much ahead but glad enough to be around stock again, free to drop things, quit if he had to, and go into the mountains at short notice. He had no serious hard feelings, just a vague sense of getting shortchanged, and showed it was all right by taking Thanksgiving dinner with Alma and her grocer and the kids, sitting between his girls and talking horses to them, telling jokes, trying not to be a sad daddy. After the pie Alma got him off in the kitchen, scraped the plates and said she worried about him and he ought to get married again. He saw she was pregnant, about four, five months, he guessed.

"Once burned," he said, leaning against the counter, feeling too big for the room.

"You still go fishin with that Jack Twist?"

"Some." He thought she'd take the pattern off the plate with the scraping.

"You know," she said, and from her tone he knew something was coming, "I used to wonder how come you never brought any trouts home. Always said you caught plenty. So one time I got your creel case open the night before you went on one a your little trips—price tag still on it after five years—and I tied a note on the end of the line. It said, hello Ennis, bring some fish home, love, Alma. And then you come back and said you'd caught a bunch a browns and ate them up. Remember? I looked in the case when I got a chance and there was my note still tied there and that line hadn't touched water in its life." As though the word "water" had called out its domestic cousin she twisted the faucet, sluiced the plates.

"That don't mean nothin."

"Don't lie, don't try to fool me, Ennis. I know what it means. Jack Twist? Jack Nasty. You and him—"

She'd overstepped his line. He seized her wrist; tears sprang and rolled, a dish clattered.

"Shut up," he said. "Mind your own business. You don't know nothin about it."

"I'm goin a yell for Bill."

"You fuckin go right ahead. Go on and fuckin yell. I'll make him eat the fuckin floor and you too." He gave another wrench that left her with a burning bracelet, shoved his hat on backwards and slammed out. He went to the Black and Blue Eagle bar that night, got drunk, had a short dirty fight and left. He didn't try to see his girls for a long time, figuring they would look him up when they got the sense and years to move out from Alma.

They were no longer young men with all of it before them. Jack had filled out through the shoulders and hams, Ennis stayed as lean as a clothes-pole, stepped around in worn boots, jeans and shirts summer and winter, added a canvas coat in cold weather. A benign growth appeared on his eyelid and gave it a drooping appearance, a broken nose healed crooked.

Years on years they worked their way through the high meadows and mountain drainages, horse-packing into the Big Horns, Medicine Bows, south end of the Gallatins, Absarokas, Granites, Owl Creeks, the Bridger-Teton Range, the Freezeouts and the Shirleys, Ferrises and the Rattlesnakes, Salt River Range, into the Wind Rivers over and again, the Sierra Madres, Gros Ventres, the Washakies, Laramies, but never returning to Brokeback.

Down in Texas Jack's father-in-law died and Lureen, who inherited the farm equipment business, showed a skill for management and hard deals. Jack found himself with a vague managerial title, traveling to stock and agricultural machinery shows. He had some money now and found ways to spend it on his buying trips. A little Texas accent flavored his sentences, "cow" twisted into "kyow" and "wife" coming out as "waf." He'd had his front teeth filed down and capped, said he'd felt no pain, and to finish the job grew a heavy mustache.

In May of 1983 they spent a few cold days at a series of little icebound, no-name high lakes, then worked across into the Hail Strew River drainage.

Going up, the day was fine but the trail deep-drifted and slopping wet at the margins. They left it to wind through a slashy cut, leading the horses through brittle branchwood, Jack, the same eagle feather in his old hat, lifting his head in the heated noon to take the air scented with resinous lodgepole, the dry needle duff and hot rock, bitter juniper crushed beneath the horses' hooves. Ennis, weather-eyed, looked west for the heated cumulus that might come up on such a day but the boneless blue was so deep, said Jack, that he might drown looking up.

Around three they swung through a narrow pass to a southeast slope where the strong spring sun had had a chance to work, dropped down to the trail again which lay snowless below them. They could hear the river muttering and making a distant train sound a long way off. Twenty minutes on they surprised a black bear on the bank above them rolling a log over for grubs and Jack's horse shied and reared, Jack saying "Wo! Wo!" and Ennis's bay dancing and snorting but holding. Jack reached for the .30-06 but there was no need; the startled bear galloped into the trees with the lumpish gait that made it seem it was falling apart.

The tea-colored river ran fast with snowmelt, a scarf of bubbles at every high rock, pools and setbacks streaming. The ochre-branched willows swayed stiffly, pollened catkins like yellow thumbprints. The horses drank and Jack dismounted, scooped icy water up in his hand, crystalline drops falling from his fingers, his mouth and chin glistening with wet.

"Get beaver fever doin that," said Ennis, then, "Good enough place," looking at the level bench above the river, two or three fire-rings from old hunting camps. A sloping meadow rose behind the bench, protected by a stand of lodgepole. There was plenty of dry wood. They set up camp without saying much, picketed the horses in the meadow. Jack broke the seal on a bottle of whiskey, took a long, hot swallow, exhaled forcefully, said, "That's one a the two things I need right now," capped and tossed it to Ennis.

On the third morning there were the clouds Ennis had expected, a grey racer out of the west, a bar of darkness driving wind before it and small flakes. It faded after an hour into tender spring snow that heaped wet and heavy. By nightfall it turned colder. Jack and Ennis passed a joint back and forth, the fire burning late, Jack restless and bitching about the cold, poking the flames with a stick, twisting the dial of the transistor radio until the batteries died.

Ennis said he'd been putting the blocks to a woman who worked part-time at the Wolf Ears bar in Signal where he was working now for Stoutamire's cow and calf outfit, but it wasn't going anywhere and she had some problems he didn't want. Jack said he'd had a thing going with the wife of a rancher down the road in Childress and for the last few months he'd slank around expecting to get shot by Lureen or the husband, one. Ennis laughed a little and said he probably deserved it. Jack said he was doing all right but he missed Ennis bad enough sometimes to make him whip babies.

The horses nickered in the darkness beyond the fire's circle of light. Ennis put his arm around Jack, pulled him close, said he saw his girls about once a month, Alma Jr. a shy seventeen-year-old with his beanpole length, Francine a little live wire. Jack slid his cold hand between Ennis's legs, said he was worried about his boy who was, no doubt about it, dyslexic or something, couldn't get anything right, fifteen years old and couldn't hardly read, *he* could see it though goddamn Lureen wouldn't admit to it and pretended the kid was o.k., refused to get any bitchin kind a help about it. He didn't know what the fuck the answer was. Lureen had the money and called the shots.

"I used a want a boy for a kid," said Ennis, undoing buttons, "but just got little girls."

"I didn't want none a either kind," said Jack. "But fuck-all has worked the way I wanted. Nothin never come to my hand the right way." Without getting up he threw deadwood on the fire, the sparks flying up with their truths and lies, a few hot points of fire landing on their hands and faces, not for the first time, and they rolled down into the dirt. One thing never changed: the brilliant charge of their infrequent couplings was darkened by the sense of time flying, never enough time, never enough.

A day or two later in the trailhead parking lot, horses loaded into the trailer, Ennis was ready to head back to Signal, Jack up to Lightning Flat to see the old man. Ennis leaned into Jack's window, said what he'd been putting off the whole week, that likely he couldn't get away again until November after they'd shipped stock and before winter feeding started.

"November. What in hell happened a August? Tell you what, we said August, nine, ten days. Christ, Ennis! Whyn't you tell me this before? You had a fuckin week to say some little word about it. And why's it we're always in the friggin cold weather? We ought a do somethin. We ought a go south. We ought a go to Mexico one day."

"Mexico? Jack, you know me. All the travelin I ever done is goin around the coffeepot lookin for the handle. And I'll be runnin the baler all August, that's what's the matter with August. Lighten up, Jack. We can hunt in November, kill a nice elk. Try if I can get Don Wroe's cabin again. We had a good time that year."

"You know, friend, this is a goddamn bitch of a unsatisfactory situation. You used a come away easy. It's like seein the pope now."

"Jack, I got a work. Them earlier days I used a quit the jobs. You got a wife with money, a good job. You forget how it is bein broke all the time. You ever hear a child support? I been payin out for years and got more to go. Let me tell you, I can't quit this one. And I can't get the time off. It was tough gettin this time—some a them late heifers is still calvin. You don't leave then. You don't. Stoutamire is a hell-raiser and he raised hell about me takin the week. I don't blame him. He probly ain't got a night's sleep since I left. The trade-off was August. You got a better idea?"

"I did once." The tone was bitter and accusatory.

Ennis said nothing, straightened up slowly, rubbed at his forehead; a horse stamped inside the trailer. He walked to his truck, put his hand on the trailer, said something that only the horses could hear, turned and walked back at a deliberate pace.

"You been a Mexico, Jack?" Mexico was the place. He'd heard. He was cutting fence now, trespassing in the shoot-em zone.

"Hell yes, I been. Where's the fuckin problem?" Braced for it all these years and here it came, late and unexpected.

"I got a say this to you one time, Jack, and I ain't foolin. What I don't know," said Ennis, "all them things I don't know could get you killed if I should come to know them."

"Try this one," said Jack, "and *I'll* say it just one time. Tell you what, we could a had a good life together, a fuckin real good life. You wouldn't do it, Ennis, so what we got now is Brokeback Mountain. Everthing built on that. It's all we got, boy, fuckin all, so I hope you know that if you don't never know the rest. Count the damn few times we been together in twenty years. Measure the fuckin short leash you keep me on, then ask me about Mexico and then tell me you'll kill me for needin it and not hardly never gettin it. You got no fuckin idea how bad it gets. I'm not you. I can't make it on a couple a high-altitude fucks once or twice a year. You're too much for me, Ennis, you son of a whoreson bitch. I wish I knew how to quit you."

Like vast clouds of steam from thermal springs in winter the years of things unsaid and now unsayable—admissions, declarations, shames, guilts, fears—rose around them. Ennis stood as if heart-shot, face grey and deep-lined, grimacing, eyes screwed shut, fists clenched, legs caving, hit the ground on his knees.

"Jesus," said Jack. "Ennis?" But before he was out of the truck, trying to guess if it was heart attack or the overflow of an incendiary rage, Ennis was back on his feet and somehow, as a coat hanger is straightened to open a locked car and then bent again to its original shape, they torqued things almost to where they had been, for what they'd said was no news. Nothing ended, nothing begun, nothing resolved.

What Jack remembered and craved in a way he could neither help nor understand was the time that distant summer on Brokeback when Ennis had come up behind him and pulled him close, the silent embrace satisfying some shared and sexless hunger.

They had stood that way for a long time in front of the fire, its burning tossing ruddy chunks of light, the shadow of their bodies a single column against the rock. The minutes ticked by from the round watch in Ennis's pocket, from the sticks in the fire settling into coals. Stars bit through the wavy heat layers above the fire. Ennis's breath came slow and quiet, he hummed, rocked a little in the sparklight and Jack leaned against the steady heartbeat, the vibrations of the humming like faint electricity and, standing, he fell into sleep that was not sleep but something else drowsy and tranced until Ennis, dredging up a rusty but still useable phrase from the childhood time before his mother died, said, "Time to hit the hay, cowboy. I got a go. Come on, you're sleepin on your feet like a horse," and gave Jack a shake, a push, and went off in the darkness. Jack heard his spurs tremble as he mounted, the words "see you tomorrow," and the horse's shuddering snort, grind of hoof on stone.

Later, that dozy embrace solidified in his memory as the single moment of artless, charmed happiness in their separate and difficult lives. Nothing marred it, even the knowledge that Ennis would not then embrace him face to face because he did not want to see nor feel that it was Jack he held. And maybe, he thought, they'd never got much farther than that. Let be, let be.

Ennis didn't know about the accident for months until his postcard to Jack saying that November still looked like the first chance came back stamped DECEASED. He called Jack's number in Childress, something he had done only once before when Alma divorced him and Jack had misunderstood the reason for the call, had driven twelve hundred miles north for nothing. This would be all right, Jack would answer, had to answer. But he did not. It was Lureen and she said who? who is this? and when he told her again she said in a level voice yes, Jack was pumping up a flat on the truck out on a back road when the tire blew up. The bead was damaged somehow and the force of the explosion slammed the rim into his face, broke his nose and jaw and knocked him unconscious on his back. By the time someone came along he had drowned in his own blood.

No, he thought, they got him with the tire iron.

"Jack used to mention you," she said. "You're the fishing buddy or the hunting buddy, I know that. Would have let you know," she said, "but I wasn't sure about your name and address. Jack kept most a his friends' addresses in his head. It was a terrible thing. He was only thirty-nine years old."

The huge sadness of the northern plains rolled down on him. He didn't know which way it was, the tire iron or a real accident, blood choking down Jack's throat and nobody to turn him over. Under the wind drone he heard steel slamming off bone, the hollow chatter of a settling tire rim.

"He buried down there?" He wanted to curse her for letting Jack die on the dirt road.

The little Texas voice came slip-sliding down the wire. "We put a stone up. He use to say he wanted to be cremated, ashes scattered on Brokeback Mountain. I didn't know where that was. So he was cremated, like he wanted, and like I say, half his ashes was interred here, and the rest I sent up to his folks. I thought Brokeback Mountain was around where he grew up. But knowing Jack, it might be some pretend place where the bluebirds sing and there's a whiskey spring."

"We herded sheep on Brokeback one summer," said Ennis. He could hardly speak.

"Well, he said it was his place. I thought he meant to get drunk. Drink whiskey up there. He drank a lot."

"His folks still up in Lightnin Flat?"

"Oh yeah. They'll be there until they die. I never met them. They didn't come down for the funeral. You get in touch with them. I suppose they'd appreciate it if his wishes was carried out."

No doubt about it, she was polite but the little voice was cold as snow.

The road to Lightning Flat went through desolate country past a dozen abandoned ranches distributed over the plain at eight- and ten-mile intervals, houses sitting blank-eyed in the weeds, corral fences down. The mailbox read John C. Twist. The ranch was a meagre little place, leafy spurge taking over. The stock was too far distant for him to see their condition, only that they were black baldies. A porch stretched across the front of the tiny brown stucco house, four rooms, two down, two up.

Ennis sat at the kitchen table with Jack's father. Jack's mother, stout and careful in her movements as though recovering from an operation, said, "Want some coffee, don't you? Piece a cherry cake?"

"Thank you, ma'am, I'll take a cup a coffee but I can't eat no cake just now."

The old man sat silent, his hands folded on the plastic tablecloth, staring at Ennis with an angry, knowing expression. Ennis recognized in him a not uncommon type with the hard need to be the stud duck in the pond. He couldn't see much of Jack in either one of them, took a breath.

"I feel awful bad about Jack. Can't begin to say how bad I feel. I knew him a long time. I come by to tell you that if you want me to take his ashes up there on Brokeback like his wife says he wanted I'd be proud to."

There was a silence. Ennis cleared his throat but said nothing more.

The old man said, "Tell you what, I know where Brokeback Mountain is. He thought he was too goddamn special to be buried in the family plot."

Jack's mother ignored this, said, "He used a come home every year, even after he was married and down in Texas, and help his daddy on the ranch for a week, fix the gates and mow and all. I kept his room like it was when he was a boy and I think he appreciated that. You are welcome to go up in his room if you want."

The old man spoke angrily. "I can't get no help out here. Jack used a say, 'Ennis del Mar,' he used a say, 'I'm goin a bring him up here one a these days and we'll lick this damn ranch into shape.' He had some half-baked idea the two a you was goin a move up here, build a log cabin and help me run this ranch and bring it up. Then, this spring he's got another one's goin a come up here with him and build a place and help run the ranch, some ranch neighbor a his from down in Texas. He's goin a split up with his wife and come back here. So he says. But like most a Jack's ideas it never come to pass."

So now he knew it had been the tire iron. He stood up, said, you bet he'd like to see Jack's room, recalled one of Jack's stories about this old man. Jack was dick-clipped and the old man was not; it bothered the son who had discovered the anatomical disconformity during a hard scene. He had been about three or four, he said, always late getting to the toilet, struggling with buttons, the seat, the height of the thing and often as not left the surroundings sprinkled down. The old man blew up about it and this one time worked into a crazy rage. "Christ, he licked the stuffin out a me, knocked me down on the bathroom floor, whipped me with his belt. I thought he was killin me. Then he says, 'You want a know what it's like with piss all over the place? I'll learn you,' and he pulls it out and lets go all over me, soaked me, then he throws a towel at me and makes me mop up the floor, take my clothes off and warsh them in the bathtub, warsh out the towel, I'm bawlin and blubberin. But while he was hosin me down I seen he had some extra material that I was missin. I seen they'd cut me different like you'd crop a ear or scorch a brand. No way to get it right with him after that."

The bedroom, at the top of a steep stair that had its own climbing rhythm, was tiny and hot, afternoon sun pounding through the west window, hitting the narrow boy's bed against the wall, an ink-stained desk and wooden chair, a b.b. gun in a hand-whittled rack over the bed. The window looked down on the gravel road stretching south and it occurred to him that for his growing-up years that was the only road Jack knew. An ancient magazine photograph of some dark-haired movie star was taped to the wall beside the bed, the skin tone gone magenta. He could hear Jack's mother downstairs running water, filling the kettle and setting it back on the stove, asking the old man a muffled question.

The closet was a shallow cavity with a wooden rod braced across, a faded cretonne curtain on a string closing it off from the rest of the room. In the closet hung two pairs of jeans crease-ironed and folded neatly over wire hangers, on the floor a pair of worn packer boots he thought he remembered. At the north end of the closet a tiny jog in the wall made a slight hiding place and here, stiff with long suspension from a nail, hung a shirt. He lifted it off the nail. Jack's old shirt from Brokeback days. The dried blood on the sleeve was his own blood, a gushing nosebleed on the last afternoon on the mountain when Jack, in their contortionistic grappling and wrestling, had slammed Ennis's nose hard with his knee. He had staunched the blood which was everywhere, all over both of them, with his shirtsleeve, but the staunching hadn't held because Ennis had suddenly swung from the deck and laid the ministering angel out in the wild columbine, wings folded.

The shirt seemed heavy until he saw there was another shirt inside it, the sleeves carefully worked down inside Jack's sleeves. It was his own plaid shirt, lost, he'd thought, long ago in some damn laundry, his dirty shirt, the pocket ripped, buttons missing, stolen by Jack and hidden here inside Jack's own shirt, the pair like two skins, one inside the other, two in one. He pressed his face into the fabric and breathed in slowly through his mouth and nose, hoping for the faintest smoke and mountain sage and salty sweet stink of Jack but there was no real scent, only the memory of it, the imagined power of Brokeback Mountain of which nothing was left but what he held in his hands.

In the end the stud duck refused to let Jack's ashes go. "Tell you what, we got a family plot and he's goin in it." Jack's mother stood at the table coring apples with a sharp, serrated instrument. "You come again," she said.

Bumping down the washboard road Ennis passed the country cemetery fenced with sagging sheep wire, a tiny fenced square on the welling prairie, a few graves bright with plastic flowers, and didn't want to know Jack was going in there, to be buried on the grieving plain.

A few weeks later on the Saturday he threw all Stoutamire's dirty horse blankets into the back of his pickup and took them down to the Quik Stop Car Wash to turn the high-pressure spray on them. When the wet clean blankets were stowed in the truck bed he stepped into Higgins's gift shop and busied himself with the postcard rack.

"Ennis, what are you lookin for rootin through them postcards?" said Linda Higgins, throwing a sopping brown coffee filter into the garbage can.

"Scene a Brokeback Mountain."

"Over in Fremont County?"

"No, north a here."

"I didn't order none a them. Let me get the order list. They got it I can get you a hunderd. I got a order some more cards anyway."

"One's enough," said Ennis.

When it came—thirty cents—he pinned it up in his trailer, brass-headed tack in each corner. Below it he drove a nail and on the nail he hung the wire hanger and the two old shirts suspended from it. He stepped back and looked at the ensemble through a few stinging tears.

"Jack, I swear—" he said, though Jack had never asked him to swear anything and was himself not the swearing kind.

Around that time Jack began to appear in his dreams, Jack as he had first seen him, curly-headed and smiling and bucktoothed, talking about getting up off his pockets and into the control zone, but the can of beans with the spoon handle jutting out and balanced on the log was there as well, in a cartoon shape and lurid colors that gave the dreams a flavor of comic obscenity. The spoon handle was the kind that could be used as a tire iron. And he would wake sometimes in grief, sometimes with the old sense of joy and release; the pillow sometimes wet, sometimes the sheets.

There was some open space between what he knew and what he tried to believe, but nothing could be done about it, and if you can't fix it you've got to stand it.

# BROKEBACK MOUNTAIN
## A Screenplay

By
Larry McMurtry and Diana Ossana
Based on a Short Story
By
Annie Proulx

For Publication
October 2005

EXT: WYOMING HIGHWAY: NIGHT (NEAR DAWN): 1963:

A cattle truck, running empty, tops a ridge on a lonely western highway.

To the east, the first faint flush of light.

Across the plain, perhaps yet some twenty miles away, a sprinkle of lights like fallen stars on the vast dark plain.

The truck roars on.

INT: WYOMING HIGHWAY: TRUCK CAB: NIGHT: CONTINUOUS: 1963:

It is lighter now, but the light is high, and the plain still mainly dark, the lights of Signal, Wyoming, vivid, closer now, perhaps five miles ahead.

The TRUCKER, inscrutable, barrels on.

WE SEE the passenger: This is ENNIS DEL MAR: about twenty, but nonetheless compelling, not light or frivolous in disposition, appearance or manner, uncommonly quick reflexes--a high-school drop-out country boy with no prospects, brought up to hard work and privation, rough-mannered, rough-spoken, inured to the stoic life. Has outgrown his faded cowboy shirt, his wrists stick well out of the sleeves, the buttons gap.

ENNIS looks straight ahead at the lights.

EXT: SIGNAL, WYOMING: MAIN STREET: DAY (LATER): 1963:

Lighter still.

The truck stops with a screech of air brakes in front of a service station.

ENNIS steps out of the truck, no suitcase, just a grocery sack stuffed with his only other shirt and pair of Levi's.

The truck moves again, almost before he hits the ground, spraying him with dust.

Tall, raw-boned, lanky, possessed of a muscular, supple body made for the horse and for fighting. He stretches.

No one in sight on the streets of Signal. After a moment, carrying his sack, ENNIS walks off.

EXT: SIGNAL, WYOMING: TRAILER: DAY: 1963:

The sun is full up, though it is still early. A gentle breeze whistles.

(CONTINUED)

CONTINUED:

ENNIS leans against a dingy trailer house, a crooked sign above the door says FARM AND RANCH EMPLOYMENT AGENCY. Smokes, waits. Sees an old pickup with a bad muffler approaching, and ENNIS becomes aware that the muffler is not the pickup's only problem. It coughs, sputters, rattles from several junctures as it pulls into the gravel parking lot of the AGENCY and dies.

The driver sits a moment in the driver's seat, then gets out and slams the door of the pickup in disgust.

This is JACK TWIST: like ENNIS, a rough country boy with little education, but somewhat different in appearance and attitude, a little less stoic, a little more of a dreamer. More welcoming, appealing, with a quick laugh. Twenty, but not as tall as ENNIS, more compact and muscular, thick, dark hair, worn jeans, bullrider's belt buckle, faded shirt, stubbly beard, cowboy hat, boots worn to the quick.

Doesn't notice ENNIS. But when he does, he stiffens a little. Looks at him--looks away.

Then the two ignore one another completely.

EXT: SIGNAL, WYOMING: TRAILER: DAY (LATER): 1963:

Eight a.m. The wind has picked up considerably.

JACK attempts to shave using his rearview mirror, an old dull metal razor and water in a tin cup. Painful work, but keeps at it, scraping away at his stubble.

EXT: SIGNAL, WYOMING: TRAILER: DAY (LATER STILL): 1963:

An old stationwagon races along, whips into the parking lot, throwing dust. The stationwagon stops about two feet from the steps of the trailer office, as ENNIS jumps up to get out of the way.

The driver, JOE AGUIRRE, middle-aged, tall, stocky, no fool, hair the color of cigarette ash and parted down the middle, foam dice hanging from the rearview, gets out. Then reaches back in for an oversize container of coffee.

JOE glares at ENNIS, then JACK, as he heads for the trailer office door.

Neither boy moves.

JOE goes inside. Door slams. ENNIS sticks his big raw hands in his pockets. JACK considers checking under his hood.

(CONTINUED)

CONTINUED:

JOE AGUIRRE
(sticks his head out the door)
If you pair of deuces are lookin' for work, I suggest you get your scrawny asses in here, pronto.

ENNIS picks up his grocery sack of clothes. Looks over at JACK. Heads inside.

JACK follows. The door forcefully slams behind them.

INT: SIGNAL, WYOMING: TRAILER OFFICE: DAY: CONTINUOUS: 1963:

Dusty, choky little trailer office. Venetian blinds hang askew, the one desk littered with papers, the Bakelite ashtray filled with butts, only one chair for guests. A pair of binoculars hangs from a nail in the wall behind AGUIRRE'S desk.

Neither ENNIS nor JACK sits.

JOE AGUIRRE, in his swivel chair, gives them his point of view.

JOE AGUIRRE
Forest Service got designated campsites on the allotments. Them camps can be 3, 4 miles from where we pasture the woollies. Bad predator loss if there's nobody lookin' after 'em at night.
(pause)
Now what I want
(looks at Ennis)
is a camp tender in the main camp where the Forest Service says, but the <u>herder</u>...
(points at Jack)
...pitch a pup tent on the Q.T. with the sheep, and he's goin' to <u>sleep</u> there. Eat your supper, breakfast in camp, but you <u>sleep</u> with the sheep, hundred percent, <u>no fire</u>, don't leave no sign. You roll up that tent every mornin' case Forest Service snoops around.

Phone rings. JOE picks it up. Listens. Frowns.

JOE AGUIRRE (CONT'D)
Yeah? No. No. Not on your fuckin' life.
(hangs up, resumes)
You got your dogs, your 30/30, sleep there.
(MORE)

(CONTINUED)

CONTINUED:

JOE AGUIRRE (CONT'D)
Last summer I had goddamn near 25% loss. I don't want that again. You...
(points at Ennis--takes him in)
...Fridays at noon be down at the bridge with your grocery list and mules. Somebody with supplies will be there at the pickup.

JOE grabs a cheap watch. Tosses it to ENNIS as if he's not worth the reach.

JOE AGUIRRE (CONT'D)
Tomorrow mornin' we'll truck you up to the jump-off.

JOE lights a cigarette. Picks up the phone. Pauses. Looks at them hard.

Awkward: they realize they are dismissed.

Leave.

EXT: SIGNAL, WYOMING: TRAILER: DAY: CONTINUOUS: 1963:

The door to the trailer slams shut behind them. JACK walks down the three steps outside the trailer. ENNIS stops, stands on the lowest step of the trailer, looks around at the bleak surroundings. JACK smiles, sticks out his hand.

JACK
Jack Twist.

ENNIS
(shakes hands)
Ennis.

A beat.

JACK
Your folks just stop at Ennis?

ENNIS
(after a moment)
Del Mar.

JACK
Nice to know you, Ennis del Mar.

ENNIS looks at the watch AGUIRRE gave him.

EXT: SIGNAL, WYOMING: STREET: DAY: 1963:

JACK and ENNIS walk down Signal's main street, headed for the bar. JACK leads the way.

INT: SIGNAL, WYOMING: BAR: MORNING: 1963:

The barroom is large and cavernous. All the chairs are stacked upside-down on the tables. It's empty except for a BARTENDER and WAITRESS.

ENNIS and JACK sit at the bar, each nurses a longneck. ENNIS peels the label from his bottle. A few empties sit in front of JACK.

JACK
My second year up here. Last year one storm the lightnin' kilt 42 sheep.
(shakes his head)
Thought I'd asphyxiate from the smell. Aguirre got all over my ass like I'm supposed to control the weather.
(drinks)
But beats workin' for my old man. Can't please my old man, no way. That's why I took to rodeoin'.
(proudly knocks his rodeo belt buckle)
Ever rodeo?

ENNIS
(reserved)
You know...I mean, once in a while, when I got the entry fee in my pocket.

JACK
Yeah. You from ranch people?

ENNIS
I was.

JACK
Your folks run you off?

ENNIS
(stiff)
No. They run themselves off. One curve in the road in 43 miles, and they miss it. Killed 'em both.
(drinks)
Bank took the ranch. Brother and sister raised me, mostly.

JACK
Shit. That's hard.

EXT: BROKEBACK MOUNTAIN, WYOMING: TRAILHEAD: DAY: 1963:

Two sheeptrucks and a couple of horsetrailers have unloaded at the trailhead to Brokeback Mountain. They are high, but still in the trees. The bleating of a thousand sheep fills the air.

The BASQUE is showing ENNIS how to properly pack a mule. Deftly hitches on two packs, as ENNIS watches.

JACK is already horseback. Several blue heelers circle the sheep.

BASQUE
Don't let 'em stray. Joe'll have your ass, if you do. Only thing, don't never order soup.
(spits)
Them soup boxes are hard to pack.

ENNIS
Don't eat soup.

JACK'S on a horse--it crowhops.

ENNIS (CONT'D)
That horse looks like it's got a low startle point.

JACK
(cocky)
I doubt there's a filly that can throw me. Let's get, 'less you wanna stand around and tie knots all day.

EXT: BROKEBACK MOUNTAIN, WYOMING: DAY: 1963:

The thousand sheep, the dogs, the horses, JACK and ENNIS and the pack mules slowly flow out above the tree line, into the vast flowering meadows of the mountainside.

EXT: BROKEBACK MOUNTAIN, WYOMING: DAY: 1963:

MONTAGE OF THE MOVING SHEEP:

Breathtaking views. Sheep grazing, dogs sleeping, Ennis and Jack tending the sheep. The sheep spread out onto the expansive treeless plain, nothing in sight but sky and land, high clouds.

1. The boys whistle, talk to the dogs as they move the sheep.

(CONTINUED)

CONTINUED:

2. Jack carries a sheep over the water as the sheep are moved uphill.

3. They continue to move the sheep on up into the mountains, dogs keeping them in line.

4. We see each of them alone in their own camp, smoking, lost in their own thoughts.

EXT. BROKEBACK MOUNTAIN: CAMP: LATE AFTERNOON: 1963:

WE SEE ENNIS and JACK setting up camp: sawing wood, building a fire, putting up the tent. JACK carries buckets of water from a stream.

Saddles are put up, horses are at rest, hobbled.

JACK hoists food to keep it from bears.

EXT: BROKEBACK MOUNTAIN, WYOMING: MORNING: 1963:

From a distance, the sound of sheep.

JACK finishes his breakfast.

JACK
(bitching)
Shit. Can't wait 'til I got my own spread, won't have to put up with Joe Aguirre's crap no more.

ENNIS
I'm savin' for a place myself. Me and Alma, we'll be gettin' married when I come down off this mountain.

Jack stands, stretches.

JACK
Shit, that stay with the sheep, no fire bullshit. Aguirre's got no right makin' us do somethin' against the rules.

EXT: BROKEBACK MOUNTAIN, WYOMING: ENNIS'S CAMP: DAY: 1963:

ENNIS sits smoking, watches as JACK mounts his horse.

Leaves.

EXT: BROKEBACK MOUNTAIN, WYOMING: DAY: LATE AFTERNOON: 1963:

Dusk on the mountain.

(CONTINUED)

CONTINUED:

JACK up with the sheep, leans up against a log, naps, a blue heeler close by.

EXT: BROKEBACK MOUNTAIN, WYOMING: JACK'S CAMP: NIGHT: 1963:

JACK, in his dark camp, lit only by moonlight, sees ENNIS as night fire, a red spark on the huge black mass of mountain.

INT: BROKEBACK MOUNTAIN, WYOMING: ENNIS'S CAMP: DAY: 1963:

Ennis whittles a small wooden figure in the tent. Looks outside at the rain.

EXT: BROKEBACK MOUNTAIN: DAY: EARLY MORNING:

JACK saddles up, in a pale world.

The mountain, misted, is the color of smoke, the high, grassy plain invisible.

ENNIS cleans the breakfast plates by the fire.

JACK mounts his bay mare. She crow-hops a little; he keeps her under control.

JACK
No more beans.

Rides off, ENNIS watching him go.

EXT: BROKEBACK MOUNTAIN, WYOMING: DAY: 1963:

JACK, up with the sheep now, holds his rifle, takes a bead on a big coyote.

Shoots.

Misses.

JACK
Dammit!

EXT: BROKEBACK MOUNTAIN, WYOMING: BRIDGE: NOON: 1963:

ENNIS finishes packing the two mules.

Steps back, looks at the mules, and shakes his head.

The BASQUE watches.

BASQUE
Something wrong?

(CONTINUED)

CONTINUED:

ENNIS
Where's the powdered milk 'n the spuds?

BASQUE
That's all we got.

ENNIS hands the BASQUE his list.

ENNIS
Here's next week's.

The BASQUE reads through ENNIS'S current list.

BASQUE
(not looking up from the list)
Thought you didn't eat soup.

ENNIS
Sick of beans.

BASQUE
It's too early in the summer to be sick of beans.

ENNIS ignores the BASQUE'S comment.

ENNIS mounts his big rangy buckskin and leads the two mules back up the mountain.

EXT: BROKEBACK MOUNTAIN, WYOMING: DAY: 1963:

ENNIS atop his horse, leads the two mules along the trail.

It is clear ENNIS enjoys the ride, the silence of the high country.

Rounds a bend--his horse suddenly balks, spooks, rears up: a small black bear in the middle of the trail across a small stream.

ENNIS is thrown, lands hard, rolls on the rocky ground.

The bear hurries off into the brush.

The buckskin races off the trail; the two mules take off, too, through the trees and the undergrowth, tearing the supply packs, scattering food everywhere. A bag of flour breaks, creating a white cloud.

ENNIS sits up. His temple is cut and bleeding profusely, blood runs down his cheek.

ENNIS gets up, stiff and angry.

(CONTINUED)

CONTINUED:

ENNIS
Come back here, you sons-a-bitches!

Stumbles down the trail after his horse and mules.

EXT: BROKEBACK MOUNTAIN, WYOMING: CAMP: DUSK: 1963:

JACK is back from the flock, hungry, looking for his meal.

ENNIS is nowhere to be found. JACK looks in the tent.

Empty.

JACK
Shit.

EXT: BROKEBACK MOUNTAIN, WYOMING: CAMP: NIGHT: 1963:

The campfire light flickers on JACK'S face. Looks around at the surrounding forest. Knows ENNIS wouldn't lag...is clearly worried. Takes a swig out of a whiskey bottle.

JACK looks up.

WE SEE ENNIS ride into camp atop Cigar, dismount, somewhat obscured by the darkness.

JACK is more worried than angry, tries to disguise his concern with indignation.

JACK
Where the hell you been? Up with the sheep all day, I get down here, hungry as hell and all I find is beans....

Silent, ENNIS walks towards the tent, fire illuminating his face. He sits on a log by the fire. WE SEE the cut on his forehead, gaping now, dried blood covering the whole side of his face.

JACK is startled by the sight of blood all over ENNIS'S cheek.

JACK (CONT'D)
What in hell happened, Ennis?

ENNIS
(exhausted)
Come on a bear.
(motions to his horse)
Goddamn horse spooked, the mules took off. Scattered food everywhere.
(MORE)

(CONTINUED)

CONTINUED:

ENNIS (CONT'D)
(beat)
Beans 'bout all we got left.

JACK hands a canteen to ENNIS, who slaps it away.

ENNIS (CONT'D)
Whiskey.

JACK picks up the whiskey bottle and hands it to ENNIS. ENNIS grabs the bottle, takes a swig.

JACK removes the bandanna from around his neck, wads it up, takes the whiskey from ENNIS, and pours some into the bandanna. Raises the bandanna to ENNIS'S forehead.

A beat.

JACK hesitates...awkward...hands the bandanna to ENNIS.

ENNIS takes the bandanna and slowly dabs it at the cut on his own temple. Winces.

JACK winces, too.

JACK
Well, we got to do somethin' 'bout this food situation. Maybe I'll shoot one of the sheep.

ENNIS
What if Aguirre finds out? We're supposed to guard the sheep, not eat 'em.

JACK
What's the matter with you? There's a thousand of 'em.

ENNIS
I'll stick with beans.

JACK
Well, I won't.

EXT: BROKEBACK MOUNTAIN, WYOMING: MEADOW: DAY: 1963:

WE HEAR a rifle shot: ENNIS lowers the 30/30.

WE SEE a two-point buck, dead on the ground.

JACK, smiling, whooping, stands behind him looking in the direction ENNIS just fired.

JACK
Ooooeee!

(CONTINUED)

CONTINUED:

ENNIS
Was gettin' tired of your dumb ass missin'.

JACK
Let's get a move on. Don't want the Game and Fish catch us with no deer.

EXT: BROKEBACK MOUNTAIN, WYOMING: CAMP: DUSK: 1963:

JACK and ENNIS sit around the campfire, and eat the venison in silence.

All WE HEAR is their chewing and chomping, and the crackling of the fire.

EXT: BROKEBACK MOUNTAIN, WYOMING: CAMP: LATE AFTERNOON: 1963:

JACK comes loping in on his bay mare.

Dismounts. Heads for the fire.

JACK
(morose)
I'm commutin' four hours a day. Come in for breakfast, go back to the sheep, evenin' get 'em bedded down, come in for supper, go back to the sheep, spend half the night checkin' for damn coyotes.
(gets a second beer, opens it)
Aguirre got no right to make me do this.

ENNIS is at the fire, dishing up supper.

ENNIS
(hands Jack a plate)
You wanna switch? I wouldn't mind sleepin' out there.

JACK
(takes it)
Ain't the point. Point is, we both ought to be in this camp. And that goddamn pup tent smells like cat piss or worse.

ENNIS
(again)
Wouldn't mind bein' out there.

JACK
(looks at him)
Happy to switch, but give you warnin', I can't cook worth a damn.
(MORE)

(CONTINUED)

CONTINUED:

JACK (CONT'D)
(pause)
Am pretty good with a can opener, though.

ENNIS
(eating)
Can't be no worse than me, then.

EXT: BROKEBACK MOUNTAIN, WYOMING: ENNIS'S CAMP: LATE EVENING: 1963:

ENNIS packs a few biscuits and a jar of coffee onto his horse.

Mounts his horse.

JACK
Won't get much sleep, I'll tell you that.

ENNIS, silent, rides off across the ground.

EXT: BROKEBACK MOUNTAIN, WYOMING: ENNIS'S CAMP: EVENING: 1963:

JACK peels potatoes for dinner.

ENNIS has only his jeans and boots on, no shirt, before a large basin of hot water, shaves.

ENNIS
Shot a coyote, big son of a bitch, balls on him size a apples. Looked like he could eat a camel.
(sloshes his face)
You want some of this hot water?

JACK
(grins, shakes his head)
It's all yours.

ENNIS pulls off his boots, then his socks.

Pulls off his jeans--no underwear.

Slops the washcloth under his arms, between his legs.

JACK fixes dinner, a cigarette dangling from his mouth.

Impassive.

EXT: BROKEBACK MOUNTAIN, WYOMING: ENNIS'S CAMP: LATE EVENING: 1963:

ENNIS sits, supper finished, his back against a log, boot soles to the fire, two empty bean cans with spoons in them nearby, a few leftover fried potatoes.

JACK has just taken a piss, is buttoning his jeans.

ENNIS smokes. Takes a deep swig from a whiskey bottle

JACK walks up, flicks his rodeo belt buckle with his fingers. Sits down across from ENNIS.

A creek gurgles nearby.

ENNIS
Don't rodeo much myself. What's the point of ridin' some piece of stock for eight seconds?

JACK
Money's a good point.

JACK finally fixes his buckle, again sits down next to ENNIS and grabs the whiskey bottle. JACK takes a swig.

ENNIS
(laughs for the first time since they've met)
True enough, if you don't get stomped winnin' it.

JACK
My ol' man was a bullrider, pretty well knowed in his day, though he kept his secrets to himself. Never taught me a thing. Never once come to see me ride.

JACK reaches over for a bean can. Begins to scrape the last beans out of the bottom.

JACK (CONT'D)
(eats)
Your brother and sister do right by you?

Throws the empty can on the fire.

ENNIS
Did the best they could after my folks was gone, considerin' they didn't leave us nothin' but $24 in a coffee can.

(CONTINUED)

CONTINUED:

A beat.

ENNIS'S tongue loosens suddenly.

ENNIS (CONT'D)
Got me a year a high school before the transmission went on the pickup. My sis left, married a roughneck, moved to Casper. Me and my brother got work on a ranch up near Worland until I was nineteen. He got married last month. No room for me. That's how come me to end up here.

Silence.

JACK looks over at ENNIS, smiles.

ENNIS (CONT'D)
...What?

JACK
Friend, that's more words than you've spoke in the past two weeks.

ENNIS smiles, for the first time.

ENNIS
Hell, it's the most I've spoke in a year.
(remembers)
My dad now, he was a fine roper. Didn't rodeo much, though. Thought rodeo cowboys was all fuck-ups.

JACK
The hell they are!

JACK gets up, does a pretend bull ride around the campfire, bucking and twisting.

JACK (CONT'D)
Yee-haw! Yee-haw! I'm spurrin' his guts out! Wavin' to the girls in the stands! He's kickin" to high heaven, but he can't dashboard me! No way! Yee-haw!

Finally throws himself, collapses in a heap among the saddles.

ENNIS
I think my dad was right.

Both laugh so hard, they almost cry.

EXT: BROKEBACK MOUNTAIN, WYOMING: LATE EVENING: 1963:

ENNIS rides into the night wind, leading the mules.

EXT: BROKEBACK MOUNTAIN, WYOMING: DAY: 1963:

WE SEE JACK and ENNIS, the dogs, the sheep moving higher up the mountain to new pasture. Both horseback. JACK leading the pack mules, ENNIS and the blue heelers leading the sheep.

EXT: BROKEBACK MOUNTAIN, WYOMING: LATE AFTERNOON: 1963:

WE SEE them pitching a new camp, more primitive this time.

JACK and ENNIS are friendlier, more familiar with each other.

EXT: BROKEBACK MOUNTAIN, WYOMING: CAMP: EARLY EVENING: 1963:

The tent is a little lopsided, but finally up. ENNIS is trying to adjust a tent pole. JACK is sitting by the fire, playing a slightly damaged harmonica, squalling out some old rodeo tune. A whiskey bottle sits next to him.

ENNIS
Tent don't look right.

JACK stops playing, glances over at ENNIS and the tent.

JACK
It ain't goin' nowhere. Let it be.
(starts up again on the harmonica)

ENNIS
(amused)
That harmonica don't sound quite right.

JACK
That's 'cause it got kinda flattened when that mare threw me.

ENNIS
I thought you said that mare couldn't throw you.

JACK
She got lucky.

ENNIS
If I was lucky, that harmonica woulda broke in two.

Both laugh.

EXT: BROKEBACK MOUNTAIN, WYOMING: CAMP: NIGHT (SUNSET): 1963:

JACK, drunk, sings a Pentecostal hymn, "WATER WALKING JESUS," a sad, dirgelike rendition, causing coyotes to yip in the distance.

JACK
(sings)
"I know I shall meet you on that final day, Water Walkin' Jesus, take me away..."

ENNIS
Very good....

JACK
(pause)
My mama, she believes in the Pentecost.

ENNIS
Yeah? Exactly what is the Pentecost?
(pause)
I mean, my folks was Methodist.

JACK
Well, the Pentecost...
(realizes he has no clue)
I don't know. I don't know what the Pentecost is...Mama never explained it.
(pause)
I guess it's when the world ends and fellas like you and me march off to hell.

ENNIS
Uh uh, speak for yourself. You may be a sinner, but I ain't yet had the opportunity.

They both laugh heartily, in a great mood.

EXT: BROKEBACK MOUNTAIN, WYOMING: NIGHT (LATER STILL): 1963:

The moon is full up, notched past two in the morning.

ENNIS is dizzy drunk, on all fours, struggles to stand.

ENNIS
Shit. I'm goin' to go up to the sheep now.

JACK
You can't hardly stand, it's too late to go to them sheep.

CONTINUED:

ENNIS
You got a extra blanket, I'll roll up out here and grab forty winks, ride out at first light.

JACK throws him a blanket.

ENNIS rolls up in it, lays by the fire.

JACK
(doubtful)
Freeze your ass off when that fire dies down. Better off sleepin' in the tent.
(stands up)

JACK staggers under the canvas, pulls his boots off, falls asleep on the ground cloth.

EXT: BROKEBACK MOUNTAIN, WYOMING: CAMP: NIGHT (YET LATER STILL): 1963:

Coldest point of the night. Fire dead.

ENNIS, outside, shivers, teeth chatter uncontrollably.

JACK looks out.

JACK
(irritable, sleep-clogged)
Ennis!

ENNIS
What?

JACK
Quit your hammerin' and get over here.

ENNIS, too cold to protest, stands, staggers inside the tent.

INT: BROKEBACK MOUNTAIN, WYOMING: CAMP: TENT: DARK, JUST BEFORE DAWN: 1963:

Both are warm inside JACK'S bedroll.

JACK is wide awake now. ENNIS, on his back, is half-asleep.

JACK, tentative, takes one of ENNIS'S big hands from outside the bedroll and guides it inside, down toward his own groin.

ENNIS, coming full awake, realizes where his hand is...jerks it away as if he's touched fire.

(CONTINUED)

CONTINUED:

ENNIS
What're you doin'?

JACK moves towards him. Takes off his jacket, unbuckles his pants.

Then ENNIS flips JACK around. Unbuckles his belt, shoves his pants down with one hand, uses the other to haul JACK up on all fours.

JACK doesn't resist.

ENNIS spits in the palm of his hand, puts it on himself.

They go at it in silence, except for a few sharp intakes of breath.

ENNIS shudders.

Then out, down, as both fall asleep.

INT: BROKEBACK MOUNTAIN, WYOMING: CAMP: TENT: FULL LIGHT: 1963:

ENNIS is awake in a red dawn. JACK is sound asleep.

ENNIS has a top-grade headache, crawls out from under the bedroll, his pants around his knees.

Pulls up his pants. Goes outside the tent.

EXT: BROKEBACK MOUNTAIN, WYOMING: CAMP: DAY: MORNING (LATER): 1963:

ENNIS has just mounted his horse.

JACK, fastening buttons, comes out of the tent just in time.

JACK
See you for supper.

ENNIS nods.

Leaves.

EXT: BROKEBACK MOUNTAIN, WYOMING: LATE AFTERNOON: 1963:

ENNIS sits atop his buckskin and rides along a ridge. Something eats at his mind.

EXT: BROKEBACK MOUNTAIN, WYOMING: MEADOW: DAY: 1963:

ENNIS is up with the flock now, rides his horse, the blue heelers running and yipping at the sheep. The flock is grazing.

One dog begins to bark incessantly. ENNIS rides over to see what the ruckus is about and discovers a shredded sheep, clearly the victim of a coyote pack.

A look of shame washes across ENNIS'S face.

EXT: BROKEBACK MOUNTAIN, WYOMING: CAMP: DAY: 1963:

Later in day, overcast. Though it's summer, there is a biting little wind.

JACK, wearing only his boots, is doing laundry. Shivers.

Squats by the stream, carefully wrings out ENNIS'S only other shirt, a denim button-up western-style shirt.

EXT: BROKEBACK MOUNTAIN, WYOMING: LATE AFTERNOON: 1963:

JACK reclines on the ground. Looks off in the distance at the grazing sheep.

ENNIS walks up. Stands. Looks off, too.

ENNIS
It's a one-shot thing we got goin' here.

JACK
Nobody's business but ours.

ENNIS
You know I ain't queer.

JACK
Me neither.

BOTH look off in silence.

EXT: BROKEBACK MOUNTAIN, WYOMING: CAMP: TENT: NIGHT: 1963:

The setting sun leaves the sky ablaze in orange and purple.

ENNIS sits by the fire, alone. Hears coyotes in the distance.

JACK is inside the tent.

ENNIS, pensive, glances over towards the tent. Decides.

CONTINUED:

Gets up.

Goes to the tent.

INT. BROKEBACK MOUNTAIN, WYOMING: TENT: NIGHT: CONTINUED

JACK sits atop the bedroll, naked, his shirt draped over his lap. He looks up as Ennis enters.

ENNIS cautiously steps in. JACK raises his hand to him. ENNIS takes it. JACK pulls him in.

JACK, gentle, reassuring, takes ENNIS'S face in his hands.

JACK
It's all right...It's all right.

JACK kisses him.

They lie back. Embrace. Kiss.

EXT: BROKEBACK MOUNTAIN, WYOMING: DAY: BINOCULAR POV: 1963:

WE SEE the main camp on Brokeback through a pair of binoculars.

Pan the camp.

Horses, dogs, then not quite in focus.

Focus sharpens: TWO MEN pulling off their clothes, out in the middle of nowhere, they play, running, joking.

EXT: BROKEBACK MOUNTAIN, WYOMING: DAY: CONTINUOUS: 1963:

WE SEE the binoculars belong to JOE AGUIRRE. He is horseback.

Looks at his watch.

Raises the binoculars--looks again--lowers them.

It is clear--from the expression on his face--that he doesn't like what he sees. Doesn't like it at all.

EXT: BROKEBACK MOUNTAIN, WYOMING: CAMP: AFTERNOON: 1963:

JACK is chopping firewood.

AGUIRRE comes riding up.

Fixes JACK with a bold stare.

(CONTINUED)

CONTINUED:

JOE AGUIRRE
Twist, your Uncle Harold's in the hospital with pneumonia. Docs don't expect he'll make it.
(pause)
Your ma sent me to tell you. So here I am.

JACK
Bad news. Ain't much I can do about it up here, I guess.

JOE AGUIRRE
(hard look)
Ain't much you can do down there neither. Not unless you can cure pneumonia.

Glares at JACK. Raises binoculars, looks in the direction of the meadow, towards ENNIS.

WE SEE: ENNIS, horseback, being an exemplary sheepman, a sickly lamb across his saddle, trailed by the blue heelers.

AGUIRRE lowers the binoculars and shoots another stern look at JACK.

Turns, rides off.

EXT: BROKEBACK MOUNTAIN, WYOMING: CAMP: LATE EVENING: 1963:

The wind is picking up.

ENNIS and JACK are gathering dishes, blankets, trying to grab their gear before it blows away.

The sides of the tent begin to buck and pitch.

Then hailstones begin to pepper down.

JACK
Aw, hell!

They both scramble inside the tent, pull the flap, but the wind whips it back open. The tent is popping so hard now it seems as if it might blow away.

ENNIS
(looking out)
Them sheep'll drift if I don't get back there tonight.

CONTINUED:

JACK
(above the wind)
You'll get pitched off your mount in a storm like this, wish you hadn't tried it. Close it up!

EXT: BROKEBACK MOUNTAIN, WYOMING: DAY: 1963:

A grim, grey morning.

ENNIS and JACK, both mounted, the blue heelers at attention. Glum, looking at a huge mass of milling sheep.

Twenty yards away, TWO CHILEAN SHEEPHERDERS are looking just as glum at the huge mixed herd, gesturing wildly.

ENNIS
What're we supposed to do now?

JACK
Get on in there...untangle them Chilean sheep from ours, I guess.

EXT: BROKEBACK MOUNTAIN, WYOMING: DAY: 1963:

ENNIS, horseback, and JACK, on foot, the blue heelers and the TWO CHILEANS work in a confusion of sheep and dust, trying to separate the two herds that have mixed.

JACK
(holds a sheep, tries to look at its paint brand, which is faint at best)
Damn, half the goddamn paint brands are wore off.

ENNIS
(trying to edge a pitiful little group of sheep out of the main herd)
We gotta try, at least we can get the count right for Aguirre.

JACK
Fuck Aguirre.

ENNIS
(frustrated, making a point)
Fuck Aguirre? What if we need to work for him again? We gotta stick this out, Jack.

CONTINUED:

JACK doesn't respond. Leans down, examines the paint brand again, drags it to where it belongs.

ENNIS resumes the weary task of separating out the rest of their herd.

EXT: BROKEBACK MOUNTAIN, WYOMING: LATE AFTERNOON: 1963:

JACK and ENNIS'S herd of sheep, reconstituted as best they can, moves along the high treeless slope of Brokeback Mountain, kept in order and in motion by the dogs.

JACK, in a better mood now, is doodling on his harmonica.

ENNIS
(tolerant, smiles)
You'll run the sheep off again if you don't quiet down.

JACK keeps playing.

EXT: BROKEBACK MOUNTAIN, WYOMING: EARLY MORNING: 1963:

ENNIS crawls out of the pup tent, shivering.

A foot of snow covers an extraordinarily beautiful plain.

Stumbles around outside the tent, trying to warm himself.

EXT: BROKEBACK MOUNTAIN, WYOMING: MAIN CAMP: DAY: 1963:

ENNIS lopes into camp on horseback. There are only a few patches of snow left here and there.

JACK is busily packing gear.

ENNIS
What you doin'?

JACK
Aguirre came by again. Says my uncle didn't die after all.
(pause)
Says bring 'em down.

ENNIS
(not sure he's heard right)
Bring 'em down? Why, it's the middle of August.

JACK
Says there's another storm comin', movin' in from the Pacific.
(MORE)

CONTINUED:

JACK (CONT'D)
(pause)
Worse than this one.

ENNIS dismounts.

ENNIS
(grim)
That snow barely stuck an hour. Besides, the sonofabitch is cutting us out of a whole month's pay. It ain't right!

A beat.

JACK
I can spare a loan, bud, if you're short on cash...give it to you when we get to Signal....

ENNIS frowns.

ENNIS
I don't need your money, I ain't in the poorhouse.

JACK
All right....

ENNIS curses under his breath.

EXT: BROKEBACK MOUNTAIN, WYOMING: CAMP: MORNING: 1963:

Their tent is struck, camp gear piled high: they have packed to leave.

JACK is tightening his saddle. Looks up.

ENNIS sits up on a hill, alone.

JACK takes his lariat, heads up the hill towards ENNIS.

JACK
Time to get goin', cowboy.

JACK starts horsing around with his lariat rope, pretends he's trying to heel ENNIS by throwing a loop at his feet--nearly trips him.

ENNIS
Hey now, this ain't no rodeo.

JACK retrieves his lariat, but throws another loop--this time, he gets ENNIS by the foot, pulls ENNIS'S foot out from under him. He falls.

(CONTINUED)

CONTINUED:

JACK laughs.

ENNIS grabs the rope and yanks hard--JACK is pulled towards ENNIS and falls, and they start to wrestle. ENNIS is only half-playing--tense.

JACK is not quite fighting, either, but the mood quickly darkens, when ENNIS slips, trying to avoid a hold, and JACK accidentally knees him in the nose. Blood pours, getting on both of them. ENNIS jumps to his feet. JACK immediately gets up, tries to stanch the blood coming from ENNIS'S nose with his own shirt sleeve, and ENNIS reflexively cold-cocks him hard in the jaw, causing JACK to stagger back and fall on his ass.

JACK looks up at ENNIS, rubbing his jaw, too stunned to say anything.

ENNIS looks down at him, wiping his bloody nose on his denim sleeve, furious and despairing all at once, more emotion stirring in him than he can handle.

Staggers off.

EXT: BROKEBACK MOUNTAIN, WYOMING: PLAINS: DAY: 1963:

They trail the sheep down the long slope, towards the trees and the waiting trucks.

ENNIS feels like he's in a slow-motion, headlong, irreversible fall.

The boys ride together, side by side, each too full of feeling to speak.

EXT: SIGNAL, WYOMING: SHEEP PENS: DAY: 1963:

JOE AGUIRRE, stern and not pleased, looks over the milling sheep.

The boys lean against the fence.

JOE AGUIRRE
(comes over)
Some of these never went up there with you.
(pause, hard look)
The count ain't what I'd hoped for, neither. You ranch stiffs ain't never no good....

The boys shift uncomfortably.

(CONTINUED)

CONTINUED:

No response.

EXT: SIGNAL, WYOMING: STREET: DAY: 1963:

Relentless wind.

JACK is in the cab of his old pickup, grinding the ignition.

ENNIS is under the hood, fiddling with the carburetor.

ENNIS
Give it some gas.

Pickup sputters.

ENNIS continues.

JACK grits his teeth...pickup starts. ENNIS closes the hood.

JACK revs the engine a few times, then puts it in neutral and pulls on the emergency brake. Steps out of the cab. Big bruise coming up on his jaw from where ENNIS punched him.

ENNIS rifles through a flour sack with his clothes and few goods.

ENNIS (CONT'D)
(to himself)
...can't believe I left my damn shirt up there....

A beat.

A dust plume rises and hazes the air with fine grit.

JACK
(squints, nervous)
You gonna do this again next summer?

ENNIS
(stops looking through the bag)
Maybe not.
(pause)
Like I said, Alma and me's gettin' married in November. Be tryin' to get somethin' on a ranch I guess.
(pause)
You?

JACK
Might go up to my daddy's place, give him a hand through the winter.
(shrug)
(MORE)

(CONTINUED)

CONTINUED:

JACK (CONT'D)
Or I might come back....
(tries for a weak smile)
...if the army don't get me.

The wind tumbles an empty feed bag down the street until it fetches up under JACK'S truck.

ENNIS
Well, see you around, I guess.

JACK
Right.

ENNIS turns to go.

JACK gets in his pickup, adjusts the rearview mirror.

Drives away.

WE SEE JACK look back at ENNIS thru his rearview mirror.

ENNIS puts his hands in his pockets, watches him go. Stands there in the wind. JACK'S pickup is soon out of sight.

He starts down the street, but before he can get a half a block, JACK'S leaving proves too much: he feels like someone's pulling his guts out, hand over hand, a yard at a time.

He stumbles into an alley, drops to his knees. Kneels there, silent, as pain, longing, loneliness, overpower ENNIS--emotions stronger than he's ever felt for another person consume him: he feels as bad and confused as he ever has in his life. Conflicted--he is angry at himself, for all that has happened, and for all that he is feeling. Punches the wall, bloodying both his knuckles.

A COWBOY passes the alley. Pauses, looks at ENNIS.

ENNIS glares at him.

ENNIS
(growls)
What the fuck you lookin' at?

The COWBOY moves on.

INT: RIVERTON, WYOMING: CHURCH: DAY: 1963:

ENNIS and ALMA--small woman, pretty, sweet-looking, young, happy on her wedding day--at the altar in a little pine box of a church.

(CONTINUED)

CONTINUED:

A FEW COWBOYS, ENNIS'S RAW-BONED SISTER and BROTHER, ALMA'S LITTLE PARENTS and LITTLE GRANDMOTHER.

ENNIS in a new jacket and a bolo tie, nervously adjusts his collar.

ALMA in a J. C. Penney's wedding dress, happy.

The MINISTER wears a plaid sport jacket.

CONGREGATION
...and forgive our trespasses as we forgive those who trespass against us. Lead us not into temptation, but deliver us from evil. For thine is the kingdom, and the power and the glory, forever.

ALMA
Amen.

JOLLY MINISTER
...under the powers vested in me, I now pronounce you man and wife...you may kiss the bride...
(wink, smile)
...and if you don't, I will....

EVERYONE titters. ENNIS and ALMA, both nervous and shy, smile, kiss one another.

EXT: WYOMING: HILL: WINTER: DAY: 1964:

ENNIS and ALMA are in a toboggan, about to slide down the hill.

They start down, ALMA squeals in delight; ENNIS whoops it up.

At the bottom, the toboggan turns over. ENNIS stands.

ENNIS
You all right?

ALMA takes his hand. Pulls him down into the snow.

Very young, they laugh, throw snow on each other.

EXT: WYOMING: HIGHWAY: SPRING: DAY: 1964:

ENNIS, in a dozer cap, shovels asphalt behind an asphalt dumper. Sweat blooms from his T-shirt collar. Sagebrush tall along the highway, swaying in the hot wind.

(CONTINUED)

CONTINUED:

ENNIS'S co-worker, TIMMY, a fat, bespectacled, annoyingly loquacious middle-aged man with a bad case of plumber's butt, works alongside him.

Talks incessantly.

TIMMY
My old lady's tryin' to get me to quit this job, says I'm gettin' too old to be breakin' my back shoveling asphalt.
(self-deprecating)
I told her strong backs and weak minds run in my family. Didn't think that was too funny.
(laughs)
I told her keeps me fit.

ENNIS, impassive, spits, wipes the sweat from his brow.

Continues to shovel.

EXT: RIVERTON, WYOMING: DRIVE-IN: NIGHT: 1964:

WE SEE ENNIS and ALMA at the drive-in. Eating popcorn.

"SURF PARTY" is on the movie screen.

ALMA has her head on ENNIS'S shoulder. ENNIS has his arm around her.

She cuddles in closer.

She's pregnant, just showing. Feels the baby move. Takes his hand. Places it on her tummy.

EXT: SIGNAL, WYOMING: EARLY SUMMER: DAY: 1964:

JACK drives through town in his truck, which rattles and sputters louder than ever.

Eyes the sidewalks and dilapidated storefronts, as if looking for someone: ENNIS.

JACK parks in the dirt lot of the FARM AND RANCH EMPLOYMENT trailer, dust and fine gravel pelting his truck's windows like hail.

INT: SIGNAL, WYOMING: TRAILER HOUSE: DAY: 1964:

JOE AGUIRRE sits with his feet on his desk, flipping through a newspaper, chewing on a toothpick. A cigarette smolders in the ashtray. Hears a knock.

(CONTINUED)

CONTINUED:

JOE AGUIRRE
Yeah?

JACK enters the trailer, the door slams behind him.

AGUIRRE looks up, annoyed.

JOE AGUIRRE (CONT'D)
(continues reading the newspaper)
Well, look what the wind blew in.

JACK
Howdy, Mr. Aguirre.
(uncomfortable beat)
Wonderin' if you was needin' any help this summer?

JOE AGUIRRE
Wastin' your time here.

JACK
You ain't got nothin'?

AGUIRRE doesn't look up.

JACK (CONT'D)
Nothin' up on Brokeback?

JOE AGUIRRE
(looks up from the paper)
I ain't got no work for you.

AGUIRRE stares coolly at JACK. No nonsense.

An awkward moment: JACK fingers the brim of the hat in his hand, looks as if he wants to say something more. Starts for the door. Pauses, turns back to AGUIRRE.

JACK
Ennis Del Mar ain't been around, has he?

AGUIRRE glares at him even harder. The wind hits the trailer like a load of dirt coming off a dump truck, eases, dies, leaves a temporary silence.

JOE AGUIRRE
You boys sure found a way to make the time pass up there.

JACK gives him a look, then sees the big binoculars hanging on a nail on the wall behind AGUIRRE'S head.

CONTINUED: (2)

JOE AGUIRRE (CONT'D)
Twist, you guys wasn't gettin' paid to leave the dogs baby-sit the sheep while you stemmed the rose.
(pause--looks hard at JACK)
Get the hell out of my trailer.

EXT: SIGNAL, WYOMING: TRAILER HOUSE: DAY: CONTINUOUS: 1964:

JACK steps out of the trailer. The door slams shut behind him.

EXT: WYOMING: DEL MAR RANCH HOUSE: DAY: 1966:

Shot of a little line cabin on a vast, high plains ranch. The little house is so alone it looks as if it sits at the edge of the world. Windy, bitter cold.

ALMA takes laundry off the clothesline. Sees ENNIS'S pickup, pulling a horse trailer, approach--it is a dot on a long, long road.

ALMA looks lonely, pretty, though dowdily dressed.

INT: WYOMING: DEL MAR RANCH HOUSE: KITCHEN: DAY: 1966:

ALMA stands at the kitchen sink, washing clothes on a washboard. WE HEAR the radio, and babies crying.

ENNIS comes in.

ENNIS
How my girls doin'?

ALMA JR.
All right. Jenny's still got a runny nose.

ENNIS heads towards the back of the house.

INT: WYOMING: DEL MAR RANCH HOUSE: CHILDREN'S BEDROOM: DAY: 1966:

ENNIS walks over to the bassinet where baby JENNY is wheezing, coughing, crying.

He picks up JENNY and cradles her.

Two-year-old ALMA JR., runny nose, gets out of her little bed and toddles over to her daddy, cries, hugs his leg as he rocks JENNY.

ALMA yells from the kitchen.

(CONTINUED)

CONTINUED:

ALMA
Could you wipe Alma Jr.'s nose?

ENNIS
If I had three hands I could....

Cradles the baby, talks to her, soothes her.

Pats ALMA JR., tries to soothe her, too.

INT: WYOMING: DEL MAR RANCH HOUSE: BEDROOM: NIGHT: 1966:

ALMA, cute and at her most seductive, comes and sits behind ENNIS, wraps her skinny arms around him.

ALMA
Girls all right?

ENNIS
(nods)
Jenny stopped her coughin'. I should take the girls into town this weekend. Get 'em an ice cream.

ALMA
Ennis, can't we move to town?
(pause--studies him)
I'm tired of these lonesome old ranches. There's no one for Alma Jr. to play with, and besides, I'm scairt for Jenny, scared if she has one of them bad asthma spells.

ENNIS
Rents in town are too high.

ALMA
There's a cheap place in Riverton, over the laundrymat. I bet I could fix it up real nice.

ENNIS
Bet you could fix this place up real nice if you'd want to.

ALMA
Ennis, I know you'd like it too. A real home. Other kids for the girls to play with. Not so lonely, like you were raised. You don't want it so lonely, do you?

ENNIS touches her breast, then moves his hand downward.

(CONTINUED)

CONTINUED:

ENNIS
This ain't too lonely, now, is it?

Hugs him hard, as she becomes excited. Begins to squirm against his hand.

ALMA
You sure the girls are asleep?

ENNIS
I'm sure.

ENNIS is on top of her now. They kiss. She moves under him.

Then ENNIS rolls her over on her stomach.

ALMA
...Ennis....

He positions himself behind her.

EXT: TEXAS: SMALL TOWN ARENA: SUMMER NIGHT: 1966:

ANNOUNCER
Let 'em rip and snort, boys! This one'll be quick. Jack Twist, hangin' on for dear life!

JACK rides out of the chute.

Comes flying off a Brahma bull.

ANNOUNCER (CONT'D)
Oh, and down he goes!

Hits hard.

The bull, angry, slobbering, is right on top of him.

ANNOUNCER (CONT'D)
Whoa, watch out there, fella! He's comin' for ya! Send in the clowns! A fine ride for Mr. Twist. Four seconds for him.

JACK rolls, gets up--then the RODEO CLOWN comes jumping in at the last second, distracts the bull, leads him safely past JACK.

ANNOUNCER (CONT'D)
Give 'em a hand, folks, our very own rodeo clowns!

CONTINUED:

The bull nearly tramples one of the RODEO CLOWNS.

INT: TEXAS: BAR: SUMMER NIGHT (LATER): 1966:

The RODEO CLOWN, a young man with something of the college athlete about him, has wiped off most of his clown makeup. Has just ordered a beer.

JACK, at the bar--watches him.

As the BARTENDER is about to bring the CLOWN his beer, JACK limps over and hands the BARTENDER some bills.

The CLOWN look surprised.

JACK
(to bartender)
Like to buy Jimbo a beer. Best rodeo clown I ever worked with.

JACK stands close to his shoulder.

JIMBO
(firmly)
No thanks, cowboy. If I was to let every rodeo hand I pulled a bull off of buy me liquor I'd been an alcoholic long ago...

There is something, a frisson, a vibe, that gives the CLOWN an uneasy feeling...although he remains perfectly friendly...takes his beer, stands up.

JIMBO (CONT'D)
Pulling bulls off you buckaroos is just my job. Save your money for your next entry fee, cowboy.

Watches JIMBO walk over, sit down with a table full of calf-ropers, all of them wearing piggin strings over their shoulders like bandoliers.

BARTENDER
(seen it all)
Ever try calf-roping?

JACK
(nervous)
Do I look like I could afford a fuckin' ropin' horse?

JACK slams down the rest of his beer. Looks around anxiously. Puts a ten on the bar. Leaves.

EXT: RIVERTON, WYOMING: PARK: FOURTH OF JULY: NIGHT: 1966:

WE SEE the little Del Mar family ease through the 4th of July crowd, trying to find a place to sit.

ENNIS, ALMA, ALMA JR. and JENNY. ALMA spreads a blanket on the ground, preparing to settle her family in to watch the fireworks.

WE SEE other Riverton citizens setting up, a few assorted rowdies drinking beer, families, couples relaxing near the DEL MAR FAMILY. Other children with their parents play nearby.

ENNIS
We should move closer.

ALMA
Let's don't, Jenny'll get scared.

A MARCHING BAND strikes up a tinny, slightly off-key rendition of "THE BATTLE HYMN OF THE REPUBLIC."

ENNIS holds ALMA JR.

ENNIS
(settling her down)
Here we go, darlin'.

TWO BIKERS approach an area just behind the DEL MAR family. Around the same age as ENNIS. BIKER #1 has a few teeth missing. BIKER #2 limps, dragging a clubfoot. Each carries a half-empty bottle of liquor. Loud, profane, already drunk. Sit themselves down on the grass behind ENNIS and his family.

BIKER #1
Woooeee...look at this crowd! There's bound to be lots of pussy on the hoof in a crowd like this.

BIKER #2
All swelled up with patriotic feeling and ready to be humped like a frog.

BIKER #1
Where do you think the most pussy's at-- Las Vegas or California?

BIKER #2
Hell, how would I know....but if you make it between Wyoming and Montana, I'd pick Wyoming in a minute.

(CONTINUED)

CONTINUED:

ALMA shoots ENNIS a nervous look.

ENNIS takes a deep breath...turns, looks over his shoulder at the TWO DRUNKS.

ENNIS
(not confrontational)
Hey, you boys wanna keep it down, I got two little girls here.

BIKER #1
Fuck you!
(mumbles to his friend)
Asshole probably stopped puttin' it to the wife after the kids come, you know how that is.

Indignant, they glare at ENNIS, as the first of the fireworks shoots into the sky, exploding in air in sync with the verse "...bombs bursting in air..." beginning the show.

ALMA
(grabs ENNIS'S arm)
Let's move, Ennis, let's just move....

ENNIS, trying to control his mounting anger, gently sets ALMA JR. on to the blanket and stands up, facing the DRUNKS.

ENNIS
I don't want no trouble. You need to shut your slop-bucket mouths, you hear me?

BIKER #2
(stands, too, faces ENNIS)
You oughta listen to your ol' lady, then.

ENNIS
Oh, is that right?

BIKER #1
Move somewheres else.

ALMA stands now, JENNY on her hip, ALMA JR. clutching her mother's skirt. Quickly gathers up the blanket.

ENNIS looks back at ALMA, then kicks BIKER #1 right in the face, bloodying his nose and knocking him out cold.

ALMA and the girls move away from ENNIS and this scene in horror, the fireworks and music in the background.

ALMA JR. begins to cry, hides behind her mother.

(CONTINUED)

CONTINUED: (2)

Several of the surrounding families are quickly packing up to get away from the brawl.

ENNIS
(to the clubfoot biker)
What about it? Wanna swallow 'bout half your teeth?

BIKER #2 has his palms raised in front of him in a conciliatory pose.

BIKER #2
(polite)
Not tonight, bud...I'd sure rather not.

Backs away, dragging his unconscious friend along with him.

ALMA and THE GIRLS stare at ENNIS, stunned and wide-eyed: they have witnessed a kind of fury in him that they have never seen before.

EXT: CHILDRESS, TEXAS: RODEO ARENA: NIGHT: 1966:

In the arena WE SEE a YOUNG WOMAN dressed in the flashiest, most costly rodeo finery, the most stylish barrel-racing clothes, on a fine, expensive quarter horse, running the barrels.

Tips one...but it doesn't quite fall...she rounds the last barrel, whipping the horse as if she's in the homestretch at the Kentucky Derby, races out of the arena as the ANNOUNCER says:

ANNOUNCER
Here she comes, ladies and gentlemen, look at her fly...Miss Lureen Newsome from right here in Childress, Texas...Oh boy...and her time is...
(beat)
...sixteen and nine-tenths seconds. Let's give her a big hand!

The words are drowned out as the crowd gives LUREEN a big hand.

EXT: CHILDRESS: TEXAS: BEHIND RODEO ARENA: NIGHT: CONTINUOUS: 1966:

JACK sits on the tailgate of his old pickup, taping his right hand for his upcoming bull ride. Hears applause.

CONTINUED:

Looks around, sees the quarter horse and the YOUNG WOMAN come flying out of the arena, everybody standing way back, giving her room.

Just as she passes JACK, her hat flies off, lands at his feet.

JACK reaches down, picks up the hat.

LUREEN trots back, patting the sweaty horse on the shoulder to calm him.

JACK hands her hat back to her. Sees a classically pretty face, lots of eye makeup.

JACK
Ma'am.

JACK looks up at her--for a moment, she allows herself to look down at him--notices his thick, dark hair, his appealing face, his sturdy body--she takes her hat, then passes on.

JACK watches her ride back to the arena.

Walks back to his truck.

INT: CHILDRESS, TEXAS: RODEO ARENA: NIGHT (LATER): 1966:

ANNOUNCER
What a heck of a way to make a living!
Next up is an up and comer, Jack Twist
from all the way up in Wyoming. He's on
board Sleepy today! Let's hope he's not!

JACK, flattered by the attention of the rodeo queen and trying to show off, hangs on to a tough, spinning bull, actually makes a fine ride.

Good dismount. Doesn't need the clown this time.

ANNOUNCER (CONT'D)
Oh boy...let's see what the judges
say...that sure looked like the winning
ride to me...

INT: CHILDRESS, TEXAS: BAR: NIGHT (YET LATER STILL): 1966:

LUREEN sits at a table, JACK at the bar. Every now and then he glances at her. Each time she is looking right at him.

JACK
(to bartender)
You know that girl?

(CONTINUED)

CONTINUED:

BARTENDER
I sure do. Lureen Newsome. Her dad sells farm equipment. I mean big farm equipment. Hundred-thousand-dollar tractors, shit like that.

JACK looks again. LUREEN is still looking at him.

This time, impatient, she gets up and comes straight to him.

LUREEN
What are you waiting for, cowboy...a matin' call?

JACK flushes.

She leads him on to the dance floor.

INT: CHILDRESS, TEXAS: BAR: NIGHT: DANCE FLOOR: 1966:

Singer sings onstage, a waltz.

LUREEN and JACK slow dance.

EXT: CHILDRESS, TEXAS: COUNTRY ROAD: NIGHT: 1966:

WE SEE LUREEN'S large, shiny 1966 or 1967 convertible. LUREEN pulls up and parks.

WE HEAR bullfrogs croaking. Radio playing

LUREEN and JACK are making out in the backseat, LUREEN on top of JACK.

She pulls back, looks him over.

LUREEN
You don't think I'm too fast, do you? Maybe we should put the brakes on.

Jack smiles at her.

JACK
It's your call. Fast or slow, I just like the direction you're going in.

She thinks about this for a second. Then she sits up suddenly, unbuttons her blouse. Takes it off. Reaches back to unfasten her bra.

JACK (CONT'D)
I guess you are in a hurry!

(CONTINUED)

CONTINUED:

LUREEN
My daddy's the hurry. Expects me home with the car by midnight.

She leans down. Kisses him.

EXT: RIVERTON, WYOMING: A & P GROCERY STORE: DAY: 1967:

WE SEE ENNIS drive up, both ALMA JR. and JENNY in the truck with him. Stops. Gets out. Takes the girls out, leads them into the grocery, clearly in a hurry.

INT: RIVERTON, WYOMING: A & P GROCERY STORE: DAY: 1967:

ENNIS, cowboy hat on, obviously in a hurry, comes in carrying JENNY and leading ALMA JR.

ENNIS
Hey Monroe.

MONROE
Hey Ennis.

ENNIS
Is Alma here?

MONROE
Yeah, she's in the condiments aisle.

ENNIS
The what?

MONROE
Uh, ketchup.

ENNIS
Thanks.

Peeks in this aisle and that, looking for ALMA.

Finally spots ALMA in her A&P smock, shelving jars of salad dressing.

ALMA
(surprised, but glad to see them)
Hi honey. What're you all doing here?

CONTINUED:

ENNIS
In a big hurry. My boss called, got to run up to the ranch...all the heifers must of decided to calve at the same time. Thought I could drop the girls with you.

ALMA
Ennis, I got a million things to do here before I can leave. I don't get off for another three hours.

ALMA JR.
Mama, I need Crayolas....

ALMA
Not right now, Alma. Ennis, you said you could keep 'em tonight....

ENNIS
I can't afford to not be there when them heifers calve. Be my job if I lose any of 'em.

ALMA, JR.
What about my job?
(gives up)
Oh, all right then...I'll call my sister, maybe she can keep 'em till I get off.

ENNIS
I may be half the night. Bring home some round steak if you think of it.

Kisses the girls. Leaves.

MONROE the assistant manager comes around the corner just as JENNY pulls a big jar of peanuts off a display. The entire display comes down, breaks, glass and peanuts everywhere. ALMA scoops her up, takes ALMA JR. by the hand.

ALMA
Monroe, I am so sorry.

MONROE
It's okay, Alma. It's okay.

ALMA
(flustered)
I'll clean it up soon as I call my sister to come get the girls.

CONTINUED: (2)

MONROE
Really, Alma, it's okay. I'll get it.

ALMA leads the girls away from the mess.

INT: CHILDRESS, TEXAS: HOSPITAL MATERNITY WARD: DAY: 1967:

LUREEN, triumphant but tired, has just delivered little BOBBY. A nurse tidies the room as LUREEN holds the swaddled baby. JACK breathlessly enters the room.

JACK
Honey, got a surprise for you.

Lureen's parents, FAYETTE and L. D. NEWSOME, enter.

FAYETTE NEWSOME
(to Lureen)
I got two whole boxes of formula for you, 120 cans.
(to L. D.)
L. D., where did you put 'em?

L. D. NEWSOME
Oh hell, backseat of the car where I left 'em. Rodeo can get 'em.

Tosses JACK his keys.

FAYETTE NEWSOME
(ecstatic, picking up the baby and holding him up to L. D.)
Oh, L.D.! I can already see who he looks like.

L. D. NEWSOME
(to his daughter)
Good job, little girl. He's the spittin' image of his grandpa...
(glances at Jack)
...Isn't he the spittin' image of his grandpa?

LUREEN gives JACK a what-can-we-do expression...JACK maintains a polite, glazed smile.

Feeling the outsider, he turns, goes to get the formula out of the car.

EXT: RIVERTON, WYOMING: DEL MAR APARTMENT: EVENING: 1967:

WE SEE ENNIS pull up in his pickup, just outside their little apartment above the laundromat. Gets out.

INT: RIVERTON, WYOMING: DEL MAR APARTMENT: EVENING: 1967:

ENNIS, ALMA and the girls have moved to the little apartment above the laundromat. The apartment is small, not fancy, but ALMA has managed to make it homey on what little money she has to work with. Clean but spare. WE SOMETIMES hear the sounds of the washing machines coming from below....

ENNIS comes in to the apartment, dusty, dirty.

TWO LITTLE GIRLS, one running, one toddling: ALMA JR., and little JENNY, eager to see their daddy. ALMA is at the stove, has made greasy hamburger.

ALMA
(stirring)
Ennis, you know somebody name a Jack? From Texas?

ENNIS, about to pick up JENNY, stops.

ENNIS
I might. Why?

ALMA
(gestures towards the kitchen table)
You got a postcard. It come General Delivery.

ENNIS steps to the table, picks it up.

WE SEE a raw-boned hand holding a postcard. WE SEE the POSTMARK, 1967, and READ IT:

"Friend this letter is long over due. Hope you get it. Heard you was in Riverton. I'm coming thru on the 24th, thought I'd stop and buy you a beer. Drop me a line if you can, say if your there."

The hand trembles ever so slightly. ALMA, busy with the cooking, doesn't notice.

ALMA JR.
Is he somebody you cowboy'ed with?

ENNIS stares at the postcard.

ENNIS
Jack rodeos, mostly.
(pause)
We was fishing buddies....

(CONTINUED)

CONTINUED:

His voice trails off.

ALMA JR. clamors for him to look at her coloring book. ALMA stirs the gravy.

The effect of the postcard goes unnoticed.

EXT: RIVERTON, WYOMING: POST OFFICE: DAY: 1967:

WE SEE ENNIS pull up outside the Riverton post office in his pickup. Gets out. Goes inside.

EXT: RIVERTON, WYOMING: POST OFFICE: DAY: 1967:

ENNIS stands at a counter, has a blank postcard. WE SEE HIM WRITE:

"Jack Twist, RFD 2, Childress, Texas"--turns it over, writes "You bet," signs it ENNIS DEL MAR, and then puts his own address on the card.

Hands it through a postal slot.

INT: RIVERTON, WYOMING: DEL MAR APARTMENT: DAY: 1967:

Gloomy, windy day. ENNIS has taken the day off.

Paces, wearing his best shirt.

Sits down by the window.

Impatient. Looks out the window down at the street, pale with dust.

The girls chase each other through the living room.

ALMA leafs through a magazine.

ALMA
(hopeful of a social possibility)
Maybe we could get a baby-sitter, take your friend to the Knife & Fork.

ENNIS
Jack ain't the restaurant type.
(pause)
We'll more'n likely just go out and get drunk.
(pause)
If he shows.

INT: RIVERTON, WYOMING: DEL MAR APARTMENT: LATE AFTERNOON: 1967:

Several beer cans on the table. Ashtray full.

ENNIS no longer paces, sits on the couch as ALMA JR. and JENNY scratch away at a pair of coloring books.

WE HEAR the sounds of a pickup.

ENNIS jumps up, looks out the window: sees a pickup slowing on the street in front of the laundromat.

EXT: DEL MAR APARTMENT: RIVERTON: LATE AFTERNOON: CONTINUOUS: 1967:

The ever-present wind blowing, dust swirls.

JACK gets out of his pickup, stiff, his beat-up Resistol tilted back on his head, holds it steady to keep it from blowing off.

EXT: RIVERTON, WYOMING: OUTSIDE DEL MAR APARTMENT: LANDING: LATE AFTERNOON: CONTINUOUS: 1967:

ENNIS has stepped out of his apartment onto a small landing at the top of the back stairs outside, closes the door behind him, as he sees JACK.

ENNIS hurries down the stairs, taking them two at a time.

Seize each other by the shoulders, hug mightily, squeezing the breath out of each other, saying sonofabitch, sonofabitch.

Then ENNIS looks around. Pulls JACK over to a small gangway. Shoves him up against the wall.

Then, as easily as the right key turns the lock tumblers, their mouths come together.

INT: DEL MAR APARTMENT: RIVERTON: LATE AFTERNOON: CONTINUOUS: 1967:

ALMA comes to the door at the top of the second-story landing. ALMA starts to open it, then looks out: and ALMA sees ENNIS'S straining shoulders. She sees them, kissing, JACK'S tilted the other direction, their arms around one another.

ALMA quickly and quietly closes the door again.

(CONTINUED)

CONTINUED:

She backs away from the front door a step or two, pale, struggling, trying to take in what she has just witnessed.

EXT: OUTSIDE DEL MAR APARTMENT: LANDING: RIVERTON: LATE AFTERNOON: CONTINUOUS: 1967:

ENNIS and JACK have pulled back from one another now and come up the back stairs and stand in the little foyer. ALMA stands in the kitchen.

ENNIS
(glad for the dim light)
Alma, this is Jack Twist. Jack, my wife, Alma.

JACK
Howdy.

ALMA
(flat voice)
'lo.

ENNIS, his chest heaving, does not turn away from ALMA, but can still smell Jack--the intensely familiar odor of cigarettes, musky sweat, and a faint sweetness like grass, and with it the rushing cold of the mountain.

ALMA has seen what she has seen, having aged years in the space of a few moments: sees her husband's turmoil...and notices JACK'S trembling hands.

Baby JENNY cries.

JACK
(trembles)
You got a kid?

ENNIS
Two little girls: Alma Jr., and Jenny.

ALMA is stone-faced.

JACK
(halting, very aware of Alma)
I got a boy. Eight months old. Smiles a lot. I married the prettiest little gal in Childress, Texas. Lureen.

ENNIS is eager to leave.

CONTINUED:

ENNIS
Jack and me is goin' out and get a drink. Might not get back tonight, we get to drinkin' and talkin'.

ALMA
Sure enough.

JACK
Pleased to meet you, ma'am.

Takes a dollar from her pocket, meaning to ask him to bring her cigarettes.

ALMA
Ennis, if you could pick me up a pack of...

ENNIS
(already heading down the stairs)
Alma, you want smokes there's some in the pocket of my blue shirt in the bedroom.

EXT: RIVERTON, WYOMING: MOTEL SIESTA: NIGHT: 1967:

WE SEE the exterior of a rundown, small-town rough country motel in Riverton.

INT: RIVERTON, WYOMING: MOTEL SIESTA: ROOM: NIGHT: 1967:

It's dark. We can make out clothes strewn around the room. The room is blue with cigarette smoke.

The two men appear to be sleeping. We hold on them for a beat. Ennis awakens, rolls over, switches on the light, pulls out a cigarette, lights it. Jack awakens. Ennis lights a cigarette for him, hands it to him.

JACK
Damn. Four years.

ENNIS
Four years. Didn't think I'd hear from you. Figured you was sore about that punch.

JACK
That next summer, I drove back up to Brokeback, talked to Aguirre 'bout a job.
(pause)
Told me you hadn't been back there, so I left. Headed down to Texas for rodeoin'.
(MORE)

(CONTINUED)

CONTINUED:

JACK (CONT'D)
How I met Lureen. Made $2,000 that year bullridin', nearly starved. Lureen's old man's got some serious money, farm machine business.
(pause)
'Course he hates my guts...

ENNIS
Army didn't get you?

JACK
Nope, too busted up. And rodeo ain't like it was in my daddy's time. Got out while I could still walk.

A beat.

JACK (CONT'D)
Swear to God I didn't know we was going to get into this again.
(pause)
Hell yes, I did. Red-lined it all the way, couldn't get here fast enough. What about you?

ENNIS pulls on his shirt.

ENNIS
Me? I don't know.

JACK
Old Brokeback got us good, didn't it?
(drags on his cigarette)
So what're we gonna do now?

ENNIS
I doubt there's nothin' we can do. I'm stuck with what I got here. Makin' a livin's about all I got time for now.

They smoke.

INT: RIVERTON, WYOMING: DEL MAR APARTMENT: MORNING: LATER: 1967:

ALMA sits at the kitchen table, dishevelled, hasn't slept all night. Nervous, a cup of coffee in front of her.

ENNIS comes through the door.

ALMA stands...confused yet relieved ENNIS came back home, struggles with complex feelings. Keeps big emotion inside. Tries to catch his eye.

(CONTINUED)

CONTINUED:

ENNIS tries to ignore her.

ALMA looks out the window...sees JACK outside his pickup, he leans against the driver door.

ENNIS
Me and Jack's heading up to the mountains for a day or two. Do a little fishin'.

ALMA
(cautious)
Your know, your friend could come inside, have a cup of coffee...we ain't poison or nothin'.

ENNIS
(as if this is explanation enough)
He's from Texas.

ALMA
Texans don't drink coffee?

ENNIS opens the hall closet. Takes out a duffel bag. Starts to pack.

ALMA'S eyes widen....

ALMA (CONT'D)
You sure that foreman won't fire you for taking off?

ENNIS takes his rod, reel and creel case out of the closet.

ENNIS
That foreman owes me. I worked through a blizzard last Christmas, remember? Besides, I'll only be a couple of days.

ALMA JR. hears her father's voice, stumbles out of the bedroom, rubs sleep out of her eyes.

ALMA JR.
Bring me a fish, Daddy, a big fish.

ENNIS
(to Alma Jr. )
Come here.

Gives her a big kiss.

Turns to ALMA.

CONTINUED: (2)

Awkward.

Gives her a quick one-arm hug, kisses her on the cheek.

ENNIS (CONT'D)
See you Sunday, latest.

Leaves.

ALMA goes to the window.

Looks out...sees ENNIS throw his stuff in the back of JACK'S truck. Gets in the passenger side, JACK gets in the driver's side.

They pull away, as Riverton comes to life.

ALMA, pale, filled with disquiet, pain, fear, watches them go. Cries.

EXT. WYOMING MOUNTAIN ROAD: DAY: 1967

From afar, the truck making its way up the mountains.

EXT: WYOMING MOUNTAIN ROAD: REMOTE SITE: DAY: 1967: CONTINUOUS:

The truck pulls up to a remote site. JACK puts the truck into park, kills the engine.

ENNIS jumps out of the truck.

ENNIS
Last one in...!

EXT: WYOMING MOUNTAIN ROAD: CLIFF: DAY: 1967: CONTINUOUS:

The boys race to the cliff edge, taking off their clothes as they go. Jump off the cliff into the lake below.

EXT. WYOMING CAMPSITE: NIGHT: 1967

Fire dying down, dinner done, ENNIS and JACK seemingly back in their old routine.

ENNIS lies back, looks up.

JACK
Anything interesting up there in heaven?

ENNIS
I was just sending up a prayer of thanks.

(CONTINUED)

CONTINUED:

JACK
For what?

ENNIS
For you forgettin' to bring that harmonica. I'm enjoyin' the peace and quiet.

JACK
You know, it could be this way. Just like this, always.

ENNIS looks at JACK, sits up.

ENNIS
Yeah? How you figure that?

A beat...JACK takes a deep breath.

JACK
(earnest)
What if you and me had a little ranch together somewhere, little cow-and-calf operation, it'd be some sweet life. Hell, Lureen's old man, you bet he'd give me a downpayment if I'd get lost. Already more or less said it....

ENNIS
(tense now)
Told you, ain't goin' to be that way.

JACK looks stricken.

ENNIS (CONT'D)
What I'm sayin', you got your wife and baby down in Texas, I got my life in Riverton.

JACK
Is that so? You and Alma, that's a life?

ENNIS stands.

ENNIS
Shut up about Alma. This ain't her fault.
(a beat)
Bottom line, we're around each other and this thing grabs on to us again in the wrong place, wrong time, we'll be dead.

Lights a cigarette, then...

FLASHBACK: EXT: SIDE OF THE ROAD: WYOMING: DAY: 1952:

LOW ANGLE - ENNIS'S FATHER leads ENNIS and K.E., ENNIS'S older brother, down a narrow trail, to the edge of an irrigation ditch. Camera is on their backs and ENNIS'S FATHER'S head is out of frame.

ENNIS
(V.O.)
There was these two old guys ranched together down home, Earl and Rich. They was a joke in town, even though they was pretty tough old birds. They found Earl dead in a irrigation ditch. They'd took a tire iron to him, spurred him up, drug him around by his dick till it pulled off....

Nine-year-old ENNIS and eleven-year-old K.E. look down at EARL'S CORPSE.

WE SEE the YOUNG ENNIS looking down at the body--as his eyes widen, WE SEE the horror wash over his nine-year-old face...

CUT BACK:

EXT. WYOMING CAMPSITE: NIGHT: 1967:

Another beat.

JACK
(white)
You seen that?

ENNIS
(flat)
I was what, nine years old? My daddy, he made sure me and my brother seen it. Hell, for all I know, he done the job.
(pause)
Two guys livin' together? No way. We can get together once in a while way the hell out in the back of nowhere, but...

JACK can hardly believe what he's hearing now...feels as if he's in free-fall.

JACK
(voice shakes)
...Once in a while...ever' four fuckin' years!?

ENNIS looks at him.

(CONTINUED)

CONTINUED:

ENNIS
If you can't fix it, Jack...you gotta stand it.

JACK
(quiet)
For how long?

ENNIS thinks for a moment.

ENNIS
Long as we can ride it.
(pause)
Ain't no reins on this one.

Both quiet.

Look up at the stars.

EXT. RIVERTON, WYOMING: DEL MAR APARTMENT: DAY: 1971:

The back of the Riverton laundromat.

ALMA JR., age 6, and JENNY, age 4, on a rusty metal swing set, impassively swinging.

From inside the second-floor apartment, sounds of an argument.

ALMA JR. slides her feet on the ground, stops swinging.

JENNY stops, too.

They listen, but can't really make out what's said.

ALMA
Supper's on the stove.

ENNIS
No one's eatin' it unless you're servin' it, Alma!

ALMA
I already promised I'd take the extra shift.

ENNIS
Well tell him you made a fuckin' mistake.

The back door swings open and ALMA runs out and down the back steps, turns the corner as ENNIS comes out behind her.

CONTINUED:

ENNIS (CONT'D)
Alma! Goddammit!

But she's not coming back. Ennis, flushed, notices the girls.

ENNIS (CONT'D)
Hey.

The girls don't respond. Awkward silence.

ENNIS (CONT'D)
You girls need a push?

They both start swinging themselves again.

ALMA JR.
No.

He pauses, nods, pauses again, goes back inside.

The girls swing.

EXT: CHILDRESS, TEXAS: SIGN: NEWSOME FARM AND RANCH: DAY: 1971:

WE SEE a sign: NEWSOME FARM AND RANCH, CHILDRESS, TEXAS.

WE PULL BACK to see an immense metal building: this is LUREEN'S father's business, where both JACK and LUREEN work.

INT: TEXAS: NEWSOME FARM AND RANCH: DAY: 1969:

Two dour FARMERS are watching JACK demonstrate a fancy air-conditioned tractor.

JACK, who can drive anything, is doing a fine job of putting the tractor through its paces, but there's an air of boyish inanity about him. LUREEN, sales binders in hand, passes behind the farmers as they exchange glances.

FARMER #1
Didn't that piss-ant used to ride the bulls?

FARMER #2
He used to try....

LUREEN looks over at the oblivious JACK, a look of mild disappointment on her face.

INT: RIVERTON, WYOMING: DEL MAR HOUSE: EARLY EVENING: 1969:

ALMA enters, puts down a grocery bag, sorts through the mail. There's an electric bill and, beneath it, a postcard addressed to Ennis. She studies the postcard, then puts it back down on the pile of mail as she hears Ennis's truck pull up.

INT: CHILDRESS, TEXAS: NEWSOME FARM MACHINERY: DAY: 1969:

LUREEN TWIST sits at a desk, smoking, clicks on an adding machine as she goes through piles of invoices. Calendar--1973--on the wall behind her shows perfect tractors plowing perfect fields.

JACK breezes in.

JACK
(brisk)
Honey, you seen my blue parka?

LUREEN
(doesn't look up)
Last time I seen it you was in it...that day we had that big ice storm.

JACK opens a closet--nothing in it but office supplies.

JACK
Well, I could of swore I left it here.

LUREEN
(stops clicking for a moment)
You know, you been going up to Wyoming all these years. Why can't your buddy come down here to Texas and fish?

JACK
'Cause the Big Horn Mountains ain't in Texas. Doubt his pickup would make it this far anyways.

LUREEN
New models coming in this week, remember...and you're the best combine salesman we got...the only combine salesman, in fact. Daddy can't drive these newfangled combines.

JACK
I'll be back in a week. That is, I will be unless I freeze and I might freeze unless I find that parka.

(CONTINUED)

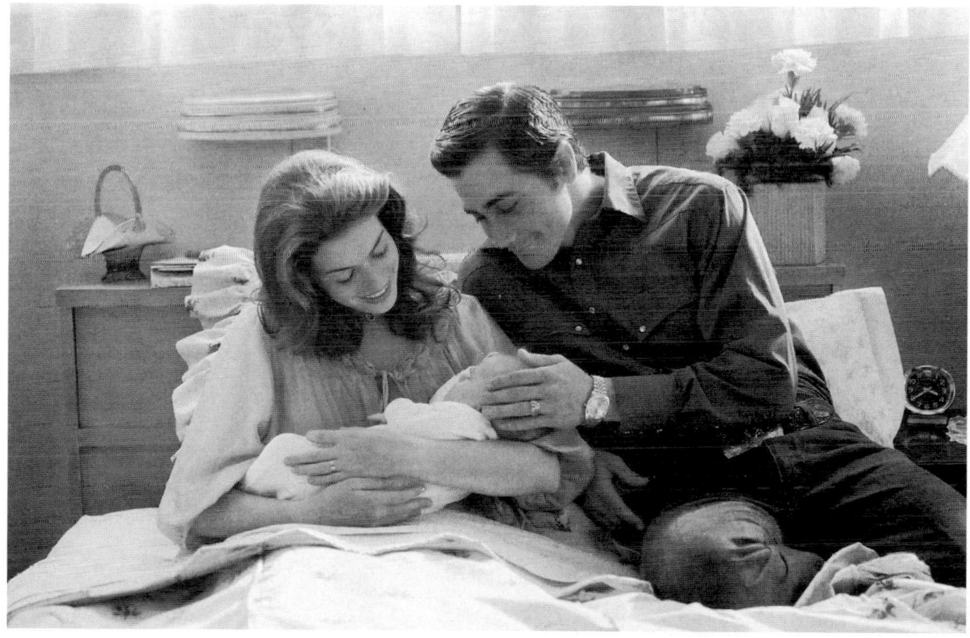

CONTINUED:

Looks at LUREEN, who shrugs.

LUREEN
I don't have your goddamn parka. You're worse than Bobby when it comes to losing stuff.

JACK
Speaking of Bobby, did you call the school back yet about getting him a tutor?

LUREEN
I thought you were gonna call.

JACK
I've complained too much, his teacher don't like me. Now it's your turn.

LUREEN
Okay, fine.

JACK gives up. Goes over, kisses her. Lips barely touch.

JACK
Gotta go, got fourteen hours of driving ahead of me.

LUREEN
(sigh)
Still don't seem fair, you drivin' up there two or three times a year, him never comin' down here....

But JACK is already out the door.

INT: RIVERTON, WYOMING: DEL MAR APARTMENT: MORNING: 1969:

Little DEL MAR apartment above the laundromat. Faint sound of washing machines coming from below.

ENNIS finishes packing for a fishing trip.

ENNIS
(to Alma Jr.)
You be good for your mama.

ALMA reads the want ads.

ALMA
Ennis...they got a openin' over at the power company. Might be good pay.

(CONTINUED)

CONTINUED:

ENNIS
Clumsy as I am, I'd probably get electrocuted.

ALMA JR.
Daddy, the church picnic's next weekend. Will you be back from fishin' by next weekend?

ENNIS puts his coat on.

JENNY
Can't you take us, Daddy? please?

ENNIS stops...looks at his daughters.

ENNIS
(smile)
All right...long as I don't have to sing.

ALMA JR. and JENNY jump up and down, clap...then reach up for good-bye kisses.

ENNIS is almost out the door.

ALMA picks up his tackle box, which still sits on the table.

ALMA
You forgettin' somethin'?

ENNIS walks over, grabs the tackle box.

Leaves.

ALMA, coffee cup in hand, sighs heavily. Inscrutable.

EXT: BIG HORN MOUNTAINS, WYOMING: CAMPSITE: LATE AFTERNOON: 1969:

Fine campsite up in the mountains. JACK'S late-model, clean-as-a-pin pickup truck and horse trailer. TWO HORSES tethered nearby.

ENNIS in his old pickup truck pulls up to a campsite.

He can see in his headlights that Jack has already set up camp. Toots the horn. Smiles.

JACK comes out of the tent, the intense pleasure of being with ENNIS all over his face.

EXT. BIG HORN MOUNTAINS, WYOMING: CAMPSITE: NIGHT: 1969:

ENNIS
Look what I brought.

Offers a small brown paper bag.

JACK weighs it in his hands, opens it: a couple cans of beans.

JACK
Beans.

ENNIS
Gonna fix 'em just the way I used to.

JACK smiles.

EXT: BIG HORN MOUNTAINS, WYOMING: DAY: 1969:

ENNIS and JACK are horseback, trotting across a high meadow. JACK fiddles with his rope. Ropes a sagebrush, then throws it at a rabbit.

JACK
I wish we'd jump a coyote. I'd love to rope a coyote.

ENNIS
(skeptical of Jack's prowess with the lariat)
I doubt I'll live to see _that_ miracle....

They laugh.

EXT: CHILDRESS, TEXAS: NEWSOME FARM AND RANCH: PARKING LOT: DAY: 1972:

JACK and little BOBBY sit in the cab of a large tractor. Little BOBBY, on his daddy's lap, steers it in circles.

JACK
Whoa, son, there you go.
(Jack takes his hands away)
No hands!

It turns and turns.

JACK (CONT'D)
It's all yours, Bobby. It's all yours.

EXT: RIVERTON, WYOMING: RANCH: BACK OF HAY TRUCK: DAY: 1972:

ENNIS stands in the back of a hay truck, looking much like James Dean in "Giant". Throws open bales of hay out to the cows.

ENNIS
Come on! Come on!

INT: RIVERTON, WYOMING: DEL MAR APARTMENT: EVENING: 1973:

ENNIS slouches in front of the television set, nursing a beer.

The girls, ages seven and nine, play cards on the floor nearby.

ALMA restless.

ALMA
It's Saturday night. We could still smarten up, head over to the church social.

ENNIS
That fire-and-brimstone crowd?

ENNIS doesn't even look up.

ALMA
(discouraged)
I think it'd be nice.

ENNIS drinks his beer. Doesn't answer.

INT: RIVERTON, WYOMING: DEL MAR APARTMENT: BEDROOM: NIGHT: 1973:

ENNIS and ALMA already in bed, kiss.

They begin to make love.

ALMA
As far behind as we are on the bills, it makes me nervous not to take no precautions....

ENNIS pulls back from her. Looks her in the face.

ENNIS
(stiffens)
If you don't want no more of my kids, I'll be happy to leave you alone.

(CONTINUED)

CONTINUED:

ALMA
(under her breath)
...I'd have 'em, if you'd support 'em....

Turns his back to her, faces the wall.

ALMA, a look of despair on her face, reaches up and turns off the bedside lamp.

INT: WYOMING COURTHOUSE: DAY: 1975:

ENNIS and ALMA in a bleak little courtroom: divorce court.

Grim.

JUDGE
...Custody of the two minor children, Alma Jr. and Jennifer del Mar, is awarded to plaintiff. Defendant is ordered to pay child support to the plaintiff in the sum of $125 a month, for each of the minor children until they reach the age of 18 years...

ALMA looks sad, but determined...cries quietly.

JUDGE (CONT'D)
(raises gavel)
...Del Mar divorce granted, this 6th day of November 1975.

ENNIS looks miserable.

EXT: WYOMING HIGHWAY: DAY: 1975:

JACK'S pickup truck races across the bleak southern Wyoming landscape after passing an ENTERING WYOMING sign. A dust devil travels across the plains, just off the highway.

INT: WYOMING HIGHWAY: JACK'S TRUCK: DAY: CONTINUOUS: 1975:

WE SEE JACK inside, happy, feeling like he could drive for days and days without sleeping, sings along with the radio playing Roger Miller's "King Of The Road". A POSTCARD rests on the dashboard of the truck. JACK picks it up, looks at it again. JACK sings along with the music with exaggerated gestures, can't stop grinning.

EXT: OUTSIDE RIVERTON, WYOMING: DEL MAR LINE CABIN: DAY: CONTINUOUS: 1975:

After his divorce, ENNIS has moved into a small, very poor line cabin, miles from nowhere, much like the one he and ALMA had lived in when his daughters were young.

ENNIS seats ALMA JR. and JENNY inside his truck. Shuts the passenger door and walks around to the driver's side, just as JACK'S truck pulls into his driveway, blocking ENNIS'S truck.

ENNIS is surprised, puzzled as to why JACK is there, but is nonetheless--as always--thrilled to see him.

JACK gets out of the truck. Walks up to ENNIS, they hug one another mightily.

ENNIS
(genuinely surprised and happy)
What're you doin' here?

JACK
(excited, holds up the postcard)
Got your message 'bout the divorce.

JACK looks, sees the girls in the truck.

ENNIS
(to Alma Jr. and Jenny)
This is my friend Jack.
(to Jack)
These are my baby girls, Jack...Alma Jr. and Jenny.

JACK looks inside the truck cab--still smiling, waves.

JACK
(back to the moment at hand, still smiling)
Your card said the divorce came through. So...here I am.

ENNIS
Yeah.

JACK
Had to ask ‘bout ten different people in Riverton where you was livin’.

CONTINUED:

ENNIS realizes now what has happened: JACK thinks, mistakenly, that ENNIS has come around, that this is their chance, finally, to be together.

The smile leaves ENNIS'S face. Rubs his jaw...takes a deep breath. Uncomfortable.

A car drives by, slows down. Ennis glances at it, nervously.

JACK looks at ENNIS...and the smile leaves his face, too. Realizes now that he's made a terrible mistake: turns pale...his body sags under the weight of disappointment. Humiliated, then devastated.

Curses at himself under his breath.

JACK (CONT'D)
...I guess I thought this means you'd...

ENNIS
(pained)
Jack...Jack, I don't know what to say.

Ennis looks at his girls in the truck. Looks back at Jack.

ENNIS (CONT'D)
I got the girls this weekend...I'm sure as hell sorry. You know I am.

JACK nods...tries to retain some dignity, caught yet again in a wrenching situation with ENNIS, feels totally powerless.

ENNIS (CONT'D)
(torn)
See, I only get 'em once a month. Missed last month 'cause of the roundup.

A beat.

ENNIS (CONT'D)
(in agony now)
...Jack....

JACK can barely breathe.

JACK
Yeah...all right.

ENNIS
Jack....

JACK
...I'll see you next month, then....

(CONTINUED)

CONTINUED: (2)

Turns away, wanders back to his truck, the postcard still in his hand.

Gets in. Drives off.

ENNIS watches him go.

EXT: TEXAS PLAINS: DAY: 1975:

WE SEE JACK blazing along in his pickup truck.

Begins to cry, hard...but something has turned inside him...he looks desolate but determined: knows where he is headed.

EXT: JUAREZ, TEXAS/MEXICAN BORDER: LATE AFTERNOON: 1975:

WE SEE a highway mileage sign: EL PASO 65; JUAREZ-MEXICO BORDER 68.

WE SEE JACK in his pickup truck crossing the border into Mexico.

EXT: JUAREZ MEXICAN BORDER TOWN: NIGHT: STREET: CONTINUOUS: 1975:

Sultry Mexican night. The street swarms with activity.

JACK wanders the streets, solemn, desperate in his loneliness.

TOURIST FAMILIES and LOCALS intermingle on the streets and sidewalks. A FAMILY poses for a picture with a DONKEY wearing a sombrero.

A swarm of LITTLE BEGGAR CHILDREN hit up JACK for change. He gives them each a few coins and moves on.

JACK makes his way through the crowded streets, entering the seedier part of the town. HOOKERS stand in doorways enticing passersby. The sidewalks are crowded with VENDORS. People yelling, Mexican polka music.

JACK turns down an alley. MEN line walls on each side. Direct looks.

A HANDSOME YOUNG MEXICAN, masculine, dressed for a night out, makes eye contact with JACK--gives him a knowing, seductive look.

YOUNG MEXICAN

...Senor....

(CONTINUED)

CONTINUED:

JACK stops. Hesitates a moment.

Then nods.

They walk off together.

INT: CHILDRESS, TEXAS: JACK & LUREEN'S HOUSE: THANKSGIVING: DAY: 1977:

JACK and LUREEN'S home. Wall-to-wall carpeting, fairly luxurious, particularly in comparison to ENNIS'S life. Many photos of LUREEN winning barrel-racing trophies. One of JACK, the one taken in the arena the day they met.

JACK, LUREEN, BOBBY, age ten, LUREEN'S long-suffering MOTHER and L. D. NEWSOME, JACK'S prick of a father-in-law. The table is set for a full Thanksgiving dinner, huge turkey and all the trimmings. As everyone shuffles into their places at the table, WE HEAR the TV in the background. Football game.

JACK is at the head of the table and has just reached for the carving tools, when L. D., older but no kinder, takes them right out of his hands.

L. D. NEWSOME
Whoa, now, Rodeo...the stud duck does the carving around here.

JACK, having been through this kind of scene many times before, tries nonetheless to be gracious.

JACK
You bet, L.D....just thought I'd save you the trouble.

BOBBY is riveted to the television set.

LUREEN notices.

LUREEN
Bobby, if you don't eat your dinner, I'm gonna have to turn off that television.

BOBBY
Why, Mama? I'm gonna be eatin' this food for the next two weeks.

LUREEN flashes a look at JACK, who then gets up from the table, turns off the television, sits back down.

BOBBY slumps back in his chair, pouts.

CONTINUED:

JACK
You heard your mama. You can eat your dinner. Then you can watch the game.

L. D. NEWSOME sets down the carving tools. Goes to the TV, turns it back on.

LUREEN
Daddy?
(pause)
Daddy!

L. D. NEWSOME
(picks up the carving tools)
Hell, we don't eat with our eyes.
(looks at Lureen)
You want your son to grow up to be a man, don't you, daughter?
(direct look at Jack)
Boys should watch football.

JACK
(stands up--barely maintains his composure)
Not until he finishes the meal his mama spent three hours fixin'.

LUREEN, BOBBY and LUREEN'S MOTHER are all startled: JACK has never stood up to L. D. like this before. They watch, silent.

Now L. D. NEWSOME stands again, goes to the TV again, but before he can turn it back on, WE HEAR:

JACK (CONT'D)
Sit down, you old son of a bitch!

L. D. NEWSOME stops dead in his tracks, his hand poised above the TV dial. Doesn't move.

JACK (CONT'D)
This is my house! This is my child! And you're my guest! So sit the hell down, or I'll knock your ignorant ass into next week....

L.D. is so startled, he automatically obeys.

LUREEN, though trying to keep a blank demeanor, is secretly pleased.

BOBBY goes on eating his drumstick.

(CONTINUED)

CONTINUED: (2)

JACK slices the turkey.

INT: RIVERTON, WYOMING: MONROE HOUSEHOLD: THANKSGIVING NIGHT: DINING ROOM: 1977:

ENNIS sits next to JENNY. MONROE sits at the head of the table. ALMA across from MONROE. ALMA JR. sits across from her daddy. The girls are about 13 and 11, respectively. ENNIS dressed in a clean Levi's jacket and a bolo tie, his shirt collar threadbare.

MONROE, at the head of the table, carves a large turkey.

ALMA is visibly pregnant.

ENNIS tries to be cheerful for his girls, not wanting to be a sad daddy.

ALMA JR.
Daddy, tell about when you rode broncs in the rodeo.

ENNIS
Short story, honey. Only 'bout three seconds I was on that bronc, an' the next thing I knew I was flyin' through the air. Only I wasn't no angel like you and Jenny, and didn't have no wings.
(smiles at her)
And that's the story of my saddle bronc career.

His girls love him, their faces rapt when their daddy speaks.

MONROE is cheerful, and a bit smug: despite his unromantic appearance, he has ALMA.

INT: RIVERTON, WYOMING: MONROE HOUSEHOLD: THANKSGIVING NIGHT: KITCHEN: 1977:

ENNIS has gallantly brought a dinner plate or two into the kitchen, sets them on the counter.

Leans against the counter. ALMA is scraping food off the dinner plates.

ALMA
(trying to start conversation)
You ought to get married again, Ennis.
(pause)
Me and the girls worry 'bout you bein' alone so much.

(CONTINUED)

CONTINUED:

ENNIS
(feeling too big for the room)
Once burned....

ALMA
(scraping)
You still go fishin' with Jack Twist?

ENNIS
Not often.

A beat.

ALMA
You know, I used to wonder how come you never brought any trouts home.

From her tone, ENNIS knows something is coming.

ALMA (CONT'D)
(trembling, but controlled)
...Always said you caught plenty, and you know how me and the girls like fish.
(pause)
So one night I got your creel case open the night before you went on one a your little trips--price tag still on it after five years--and I tied a note on the end of the line. It said, 'Hello, Ennis, bring some fish home, love, Alma'...
(pause)
...And then you come back lookin' all perky and said you'd caught a bunch a browns and ate them up. Do you remember?

Looks over at ENNIS, stiff.

ALMA is scraping harder and faster, as if she means to take the pattern off the plates.

ALMA (CONT'D)
I looked in the case first chance I got and there was my note still tied there.

ALMA turns on the water in the sink, sluices the plates.

ENNIS
That don't mean nothin', Alma.

ALMA
(turns on him)
Don't try to fool me no more, Ennis, I know what it means. Jack Twist?

CONTINUED: (2)

ENNIS
Alma...

ALMA
Jack Nasty. You didn't go up there to fish. You and him....

ENNIS grabs her wrist and twists it.

ENNIS
Now you listen to me, you don't know nothin' about it.

Tears spring to her eyes, she drops a dish.

ALMA
I'm goin' to yell for Monroe.

ENNIS
Go on and fuckin' yell. I'll make him eat the fuckin' floor and you, too.

Lets go.

ALMA
(crying)
Get out, get out, get out!
(between sobs)
Get out of my house, Ennis Del Mar! You hear me? You get out!

ALMA is crying hard now, years of pain and anger welling up and spilling over.

INT: RIVERTON, WYOMING: MONROE HOUSEHOLD: LIVING ROOM: THANKSGIVING NIGHT: CONTINUOUS: 1977:

ENNIS takes the living room in about two strides, ignoring the startled MONROE, who is smoking a cheap after-dinner cigar.

ENNIS grabs his hat, shoves it on, when little JENNY yells

JENNY
Daddy!

ENNIS slams out.

EXT: RIVERTON, WYOMING: MONROE HOUSE: THANKSGIVING NIGHT: CONTINUOUS: 1977:

Snowing. JENNY and ALMA JR., confused, a little frantic now, wanting it to be all right again, follow their daddy out on to the front stoop of the little frame house.

JENNY AND ALMA JR.
'Bye, Daddy....

Gets to his old battered pickup--gets in, bales of hay collecting snow in the truck bed.

They watch as his truck rumbles away.

EXT: DOWNTOWN RIVERTON, WYOMING: BLACK AND BLUE EAGLE BAR: NIGHT: 1977:

ENNIS parks across the street from the BLACK AND BLUE EAGLE BAR.

Gets out and without looking or bothering about the thin traffic, walks across the street towards the bar.

A pickup with a roughneck in it has to brake sharply to keep from hitting him.

FIRST ROUGHNECK
(driving, size of a bear)
Hey, asshole, watch where you're goin'!

Without hesitation, ENNIS runs around the pickup, punches right inside the open driver window four or five times. Then yanks open the driver door, drags the huge man out in the slushy street, pummelling him and kicking him.

Knees him in the nuts.

But the roughneck throws him to the ground. Punches him in the face, stomach. Doesn't let up.

EXT: WYOMING MOUNTAINS: DAY: 1978:

JACK and ENNIS ride through the mountains, like Randolph Scott and Joel McCrea in "Ride The High Country," only more life-worn, more weather-beaten.

Cross a river on their horses.

EXT: WYOMING MOUNTAINS: DAY: 1978:

Washing tin plates.

(CONTINUED)

CONTINUED:

JACK is a little thicker around the haunch.

JACK
All I'm sayin' is, what's the point to makin' it? If the taxes don't get it, the inflation eats it all up. You should see Lureen, punchin' numbers into her adding machine, huntin' for extra zeros, her eyes gettin' smaller and smaller, it's like watchin' a rabbit tryin' to squeeze into a snakehole with a coyote on its tail.

ENNIS
High-class entertainment.

JACK
For what it's worth.

ENNIS
Lureen. You and her, it's normal and all?

JACK
Sure.

ENNIS
And she don't ever suspect?

JACK shakes his head no.

ENNIS (CONT'D)
You ever get the feelin', I don't know, when you're in town, and someone looks at you, suspicious...like he <u>knows</u>. And then you get out on the pavement, and everyone, lookin' at you, and maybe they all know too?

JACK
Maybe it's time you moved outta there. You know, set yourself up somewhere different. Maybe Texas.

ENNIS
Texas? Sure, and maybe you'll convince Alma to let you and Lureen adopt my girls, and then we could all live together, herding sheep, and it'll just rain money from L. D. Newsome, and whiskey'll flow in the streams....

CONTINUED: (2)

JACK
Aw, go to hell, Ennis del Mar. You want to live your miserable fuckin' life, go right ahead. I was just thinkin' out loud.

He marches off.

ENNIS
You're a real thinker, ain't you!
(to himself)
Yeah, that Jack Twist, he's got it all figured out, ain't you?

INT: RIVERTON, WYOMING: WOLF EARS BAR: NIGHT: 1978:

The bar is moderately crowded with COWBOYS and their WOMEN. Not a wild scene.

A few COUPLES dance on the small floor near the jukebox. The TV above the bar is on.

ENNIS sits at a table by himself, a few empties in front of him.

The song ends.

The waitress, CASSIE, mid-twenties, livelier than ALMA, very appealing, curvy in jeans and T-shirt, struts past ENNIS'S booth to the jukebox, a glass of white wine in her hand.

CASSIE has her eye on ENNIS, who is oblivious, looking up at the TV.

CASSIE pops a quarter in the jukebox.

ENNIS gets up from his booth and starts towards the men's room.

Steve Earle's "DEVIL'S RIGHT HAND" begins to play on the jukebox.

CASSIE seizes the opportunity, steps in front of ENNIS.

CASSIE
(appealing, direct)
Just finished my shift. Wanna dance?

ENNIS looks past CASSIE to the men's room door.

CONTINUED:

ENNIS
(pointing over CASSIE'S shoulder to the men's room)
Was on my way to the...

CASSIE
(grabs ENNIS'S pointing finger)
I'm Cassie...Cassie Cartwright.

CASSIE takes a reluctant ENNIS by the finger and leads him to the little dance floor, setting her wineglass down on the way.

ENNIS
(being pulled)
Ennis del Mar.

CASSIE and ENNIS are the only people on the dance floor.

It is immediately clear that ENNIS cannot dance. But CASSIE doesn't mind, makes the most of the moment, enjoys herself, shaking the funk out of her ass, letting her hair fly.

During the chorus, CASSIE'S and ENNIS'S eyes meet.

It is obvious ENNIS appeals to her.

INT: RIVERTON, WYOMING: WOLF EARS BAR: NIGHT: CONTINUOUS: 1978:

The dance ends; they return to ENNIS'S table. He lights a cigarette.

CASSIE sits down across from ENNIS. Drinks her white wine. The WAITRESS comes over, refills her glass from a cheap bottle with a screw lid. CASSIE motions to her to leave the bottle.

ENNIS
No more dancin' for me.
(a beat)
I hope.

CASSIE
You're safe. My feet hurt.

CASSIE takes her shoes off, starts rubbing her feet.

ENNIS looks on, amused.

ENNIS
Hard work, is it?

(CONTINUED)

CONTINUED:

CASSIE
(playful)
Yeah, drunks like you demanding beer after beer, smoking. Gets tiresome.
(beat)
What do you do, Ennis del Mar?

ENNIS
Well, earlier today I was castratin' calves.

CASSIE wrinkles up her nose, shivers, then thrusts her stocking feet into ENNIS'S lap.

ENNIS is startled.

ENNIS (CONT'D)
What are you doin'?

CASSIE
(smiles)
Tryin' to get a foot rub, dummy.

ENNIS smiles back.

INT: CHILDRESS, TEXAS: DANCE HALL: NIGHT: 1978:

Big banner over the stage: "1978 BENEFIT FOR THE CHILDRESS COUNTY CHILDREN'S HOME." The band fiddles away, lots of couples on the dance floor.

The TWISTS and the MALONES are at a table near the dance floor. LUREEN is smoking, bored. LASHAWN has on a flashy cocktail dress, a lot of makeup and jewelry, but much prettier than LUREEN, skinnier, perky, about thirty. Restless, impatient.

LASHAWN
(chatters like a squirrel)
Pledged Tri Delt at SMU and I sure never thought I'd end up in a pokey little place like Childress, but then I met Randall at an Aggie game, and he was an animal husbandry major, and we been here a month, he got the foreman job over at Roy Taylor's ranch. Like it or not, here I am!

LUREEN
(briefly stirs)
Oh, you was Tri Delt? I was Kappa Phi myself.

(CONTINUED)

CONTINUED:

LASHAWN
(impatient)
Well, even though we ain't quite sorority sisters, we may have to dance with ourselves, Lureen. Our husbands ain't the least bit interested in dancin', they don't seem to have a smidgin of rhythm between 'em.

LUREEN
It's funny, ain't it? Husbands don't never seem to dance with their wives.
(sarcastic)
Why do you think that is, Jack?

JACK wants to have a good time--doesn't take her bait.

JACK
Ain't never give it a thought.
(to Lashawn)
Wanna dance?

They get up, go to the dance floor, begin to dance.

LASHAWN
(chatters like a squirrel)
Thank you for asking to dance with me, I really appreciate that, I really do. It's a good thing that you and Lureen happened along when you did, or else we'd still be stuck on the side of the road in that dern pickup. I told Randall we oughta take the car, 'course he don't ever listen to me. He wouldn't listen to me if he was goin' deaf tomorrow. I told Randall it takes more than chewing gum and baling wire to keep a pickup goin'.

JACK nods politely, but is looking over her shoulder at LUREEN and RANDALL. LUREEN smokes. RANDALL studies JACK and LASHAWN on the dance floor.

LASHAWN (CONT'D)
...Well, he's never been very mechanical, though....

EXT: CHILDRESS, TEXAS: DANCE HALL: NIGHT (LATER): 1978:

JACK and RANDALL sit together outside the dance hall, waiting for their wives to return from the ladies' room. Both smoke.

CONTINUED:

JACK
Ever notice how a woman'll powder her nose before a party starts, and then powder it again when the party's over?
(pause)
Why powder your nose just to go home to bed?

RANDALL
(as if the vanity of women is a tiresome subject)
Don't know.
(smokes)
Even if I wanted to know, couldn't get a word in with Lashawn long enough to ask. Woman talks a blue streak.

JACK
Lively little gal.
(pause)
You'll like working for Roy Taylor. He's solid.

RANDALL
Yeah. Roy, he's a good ole boy.

A beat.

RANDALL (CONT'D)
He's got a little cabin down on Lake Kemp. Got a croppie house...little boat. Said I can use it whenever I want.
(pause)
We ought to go down there some weekend. Drink a little whiskey, fish some. Get away, you know?

Before JACK can respond, the WOMEN come out, hurrying, LASHAWN talking a blue streak, just like RANDALL said.

LASHAWN
...when I was right out of SMU I coulda had my pick of pretty much any job in North Dallas, so my pick was Neiman Marcus which was a disaster because where clothes is concerned, honey, I got no resistance, I was spending more than I made, more probably than Randall ever will make...we come out here thinking ranching was still big hats and Marlboros, boy, were we behind the times....

EXT: RIVERTON, WYOMING: MONROE HOUSE: MID MORNING: 1979:

ALMA JR., fifteen now, waits, sits on the stoop.

Rises as ENNIS'S truck pulls up, excited.

Sees CASSIE in the passenger seat. Her face falls a bit, but she puts on a good show as her father emerges from the truck and walks towards her.

ENNIS
Hey there Junior, you ready?

She looks past him towards the truck.

ALMA JR. smiles at her father, a weak smile.

INT: RIVERTON, WYOMING: WOLF EARS BAR: LATER IN DAY: 1979:

ENNIS at the jukebox, stuffing quarters.

CASSIE and ALMA JR. at the table, watch him from across the room.

CASSIE
What do you think? Your daddy ever gonna see fit to settle down again?

ALMA JR. doesn't want to respond.

ALMA JR.
Don't know.
(pause)
Maybe Daddy's not the marrying kind.

CASSIE
You don't think so? Or you don't think I'm the one for him?

ALMA JR.
(shrug)
You're good enough.

CASSIE can't help but laugh.

CASSIE
You don't talk much, but you get your point across.

ALMA JR.
(embarrassed at how rude she's been)
I'm sorry. I didn't mean to be rude.

(CONTINUED)

CONTINUED:

ENNIS rejoins them. CASSIE leaps up.

CASSIE
C'mon cowboy, you're stayin' on your feet.

ENNIS looks at ALMA JR.

ALMA JR. nurses a coke at the table. Pensive, watches CASSIE and ENNIS dance.

INT./EXT. RIVERTON, WYOMING: ENNIS'S TRUCK: DUSK: 1979:

ENNIS drives ALMA JR. home.

ENNIS
I'll pick you and Jenny up next weekend after church.

ALMA JR.
Fine.

ENNIS
You all right?

ALMA JR.
Yes.

ENNIS
Sure?

ALMA JR.
Daddy. I was thinking, what with the new baby and all...Ma and Monroe, they've been awful strict on me. More on me than on Jenny even.
(pause)
I was thinking, maybe I could...maybe I could come stay with you, Daddy...I'd be a big help to you, I know I would.

ENNIS
Now honey, you know I ain't really set up for that. And with the roundup coming, I won't ever be home.

Pulls up to the house.

ALMA JR.
(sags)
It's all right, Daddy.

CONTINUED:

ENNIS
I ain't saying I wouldn't want...

ALMA JR.
No, it's all right. I understand..

ENNIS
See you next Sunday, then.

ALMA JR.
Bye.

ENNIS
Bye, sweetheart.

She pushes her door open; he watches her jog up to the house, then starts the truck, pulls out.

EXT: WYOMING MOUNTAINS: LAKE: CAMP: NIGHT (LATER): 1981:

ENNIS and JACK are sitting around the campfire, close.

JACK rolls a joint.

JACK is restless. Pokes at the fire with a stick. Looks up at the night sky, clouds churning past the moon.

JACK
It's gonna snow tonight for sure.
(look)
All this time, and you ain't found nobody else to marry?

JACK lights the joint, takes a drag.

ENNIS
(noncommittal)
Been puttin' the blocks to a good-lookin' little gal over in Riverton. Waitresses part-time, wants to go to nursing school.

JACK passes it to ENNIS.

Now ENNIS gives JACK a look--there is still much uncharted territory between them.

ENNIS (CONT'D)
What about you and Lureen?

Takes a hit. Passes it back to JACK.

(CONTINUED)

CONTINUED:

JACK
Lureen's good at makin' hard deals in the machinery business, but so far as our marriage goes, we could do it over the phone.
(passes it back to Ennis)
I kinda got a thing goin' with a ranch foreman's wife over in Childress. Expect to get shot by Lureen or the husband one, ever' time I slip off to see her.

ENNIS
(laughs)
Probably deserve it.

They both laugh...then the laughter trails off.

A beat.

JACK
(looks at Ennis)
Tell you what...truth is, sometimes I miss you so bad I can hardly stand it...

They both look into the fire.

INT. WYOMING MOUNTAINS: TENT: EARLY MORNING: 1981:

The two men, asleep in the tent, ENNIS curled around JACK.

EXT: WYOMING MOUNTAINS: TRAILHEAD: MORNING: 1981:

JACK and ENNIS have loaded the horses into a trailer hitched to ENNIS'S pickup truck.

Mood between them is tense, as always, when their time together is about to end.

When the gate is shut on the horses, JACK pops his glove against his leg a time or two...looks at ENNIS, who is lighting a cigarette.

JACK
Guess I'll head on up to Lightnin' Flat. See the folks for a day or two.

ENNIS
(uncomfortable)
Somethin' I been meanin' to tell you, bud. It's likely November before I can get away again, after we ship stock and before the winter feedin' starts.

CONTINUED:

JACK
(stunned)
November? What in hell happened to August? Christ, Ennis, you had a fuckin' week to say some little word about this.

ENNIS is silent.

JACK (CONT'D)
And why's it we're always in the friggin' cold weather? We oughta go south, where it's warm. We oughta go to Mexico.

ENNIS
Mexico?
(tries to lighten the mood)
Hell...you know me. 'Bout all the travelin' I ever done is goin' around the coffeepot, lookin' for the handle.

An uncomfortable silence.

ENNIS (CONT'D)
Lighten up on me, Jack. We can hunt in November, kill a nice elk. Try if I can get Don Wroe's cabin again. We had a good time that year, didn't we?

A beat.

JACK starts popping his glove on his leg again.

JACK
(bitter disappointment)
Never enough time, never enough.
(looks at Ennis)
You know, friend, this is a goddamn bitch of a unsatisfactory situation. You used to come away easy. Now it's like seein' the Pope.

ENNIS
Jack, I got to work. Them earlier days I used to quit the jobs. You forget how it is, bein' broke all the time. You ever hear of child support? Let me tell you, I can't quit this one. And I can't get the time off.
(pause)
Was tough enough gettin' this time. The trade-off was August.
(pause)
You got a better idea?

(CONTINUED)

CONTINUED: (2)

JACK
(bitter, accusatory)
I did, once.

ENNIS says nothing. Straightens up slowly, rubs at his forehead. Walks to the horse trailer, says something that only the horses can hear. Turns and walks back to JACK at a deliberate pace.

Mexico was THE place--ENNIS has heard.

ENNIS
You been to Mexico, Jack? I heard about what they got in Mexico for boys like you.

JACK, braced for it all these years, and here it comes, late and unexpected.

JACK
Hell yes, I been to Mexico. Is that a fuckin' problem?

ENNIS
I got a say this to you one time, Jack fuckin' Twist. And I ain't foolin'. What I don't know, all them things I don't know...could get you killed if I should come to know them.

JACK
Try this one...
(pause)
...and I'll say it just one time.

ENNIS
Go ahead!

JACK
Tell you what, we could of had a good life together, a fuckin' real good life, had us a place of our own. You wouldn't do it, Ennis, so what we got now is Brokeback Mountain. Everything built on that. It's all we got, boy, fuckin' all, so I hope you know that if you don't never know the rest. Count the damn few times we been together in nearly twenty years. Measure the fuckin' short leash you keep me on, then ask me about Mexico and then tell me you'll kill me for needin' somethin' I don't hardly never get. You got no idea how bad it gets.
(MORE)

CONTINUED: (3)

JACK (CONT'D)
I'm not you. I can't make it on a couple of high-altitude fucks once or twice a year.
(pause)
You're too much for me, Ennis, you son of a whoreson bitch.
(pause)
I wish I knew how to quit you.

WE PULL BACK NOW.

Like vast clouds of steam from thermal springs in winter, the years of things unsaid and now unsayable--admissions, declarations, shames, guilts, fears--rise around them.

ENNIS stands as if heartshot, face gray and deep-lined. Fights a silent battle, grimaces.

ENNIS
Then why don't you?! Why don't you let me be? It's because of you, Jack, that I'm like this. I'm nothin'. I'm nowhere.

JACK starts towards him, but ENNIS jerks away.

ENNIS (CONT'D)
Get the fuck off me!

JACK moves towards him again, and this time, ENNIS doesn't resist.

JACK
Come here...It's all right. It's all right...damn you, Ennis.

And then...they hug one another, a fierce, desperate embrace--managing to torque things almost to where they had been, for what they've just said is no news: as always, nothing ended, nothing begun, nothing resolved.

CUT TO FLASHBACK: EXT: BROKEBACK MOUNTAIN, WYOMING: CAMPFIRE: NIGHT: CONTINUOUS: 1963:

JACK and ENNIS, much younger.

JACK and ENNIS have finished the last meal of the day. JACK stands by the campfire, warming himself. He stands that way for a few moments, alone.

Then WE SEE two arms encircle him from behind: it is ENNIS.

They stand that way for a moment, JACK leaning back into ENNIS.

(CONTINUED)

CONTINUED:

ENNIS'S breath comes slow and quiet, then he starts to gently rock back and forth a little, lit by the warm fire tossing ruddy chunks of light, the shadow of their bodies a single column against a rock. ENNIS hums quietly.

Nothing mars this moment for JACK, even though he knows that ENNIS does not embrace him face to face because he does not want to see or feel that it is JACK he holds--because for now, they are wrapped in a closeness that satisfies some shared and sexless hunger, that is not really sleep but something else drowsy and tranced--until ENNIS, dredging up a rusty phrase from the childhood time before his mother died, says:

ENNIS
Come on now, you're sleepin' on your feet like a horse.
(pause)
My mama used to say that to me when I was little....

They stand like that for another moment.

ENNIS (CONT'D)
...and sing to me....

ENNIS sings low, a childhood song, from some long-ago memory.

ENNIS (CONT'D)
I got to go.

Gives JACK a little shake, a gentle push, and JACK stumbles ever so slightly in the direction of his tent. Stops.

Hears ENNIS'S spurs jingle as he mounts his horse.

ENNIS (CONT'D)
...See you in the mornin'....

A shuddering snort from ENNIS'S horse, the grind of hoof on stone, and ENNIS rides away, a very young JACK watching him go.

CUT TO EXT: WYOMING MOUNTAINS: TRAILHEAD: MORNING: PRESENT: CONTINUOUS: 1981:

WE ARE BACK TO THE PRESENT as JACK, much older now, watches the pickup truck, and his other half, fade away into the distance, that dozy embrace solidified in his memory as the single moment of artless, charmed happiness in their separate and difficult lives.

INT: RIVERTON, WYOMING: DENNY'S RESTAURANT: NIGHT: 1981:

ENNIS sits in a booth, eating a slice of apple pie and drinking coffee.

Enter CASSIE accompanied by a good-looking, decent guy. They're smiling at some shared joke. CASSIE catches ENNIS out of the corner of her eye. She says something to the man, comes over to Ennis, slips into the booth across the table from him.

CASSIE
(fake cheerful)
Hey Ennis del Mar. Where you been?

ENNIS
Here and there.

CASSIE
(quieter)
I left word for you with Steve at the ranch. And you must of got those notes I left at your place.

ENNIS
(glances at the man)
Looks like I got the message, in any case.

CASSIE
(looking back)
Carl? Yeah, Carl's nice. He even talks.

A pause.

ENNIS
Well then, good for you.

She gets up.

CASSIE
Yeah, well, good for me.

Drops herself back down, anger rising.

CASSIE (CONT'D)
I don't get you, Ennis del Mar.

Knows he's hurt her, but he doesn't know what to do about it. The look on his face changes then, to a look of stark loneliness. She knows she's not the answer.

(CONTINUED)

CONTINUED:

ENNIS
I'm sorry.
(pause)
Was probably no fun anyway, was I?

She gets up.

CASSIE
(anguished whisper, on verge of tears)
Oh, Ennis...girls don't fall in love with fun!

Starts crying as she rushes off to CARL, who waits by the door. CARL looks back at ENNIS; ENNIS shoots CARL a murderous look. CARL hurries CASSIE outside.

ENNIS stares out the window as they get in CARL'S car, speed off.

Miserable.

EXT: RIVERTON, WYOMING: POST OFFICE: DAY: 1982:

ENNIS comes out of the little post office, casually shuffling through a handful of mail. Stock magazines, a flyer advertising a big sale at the grocery store.

Stops: there is a postcard with his own handwriting on it, addressed to Jack Twist, RFD 2, Childress, Texas.

Across the address, stamped in red: DECEASED.

EXT: RIVERTON, WYOMING: PAY TELEPHONE: DAY: 1982:

A windy day, dust swirls.

ENNIS is dialing the telephone.

SPLIT SCREEN: ENNIS STANDING OUTSIDE, RIVERTON, WYOMING, COVERS ONE EAR/LUREEN TWIST'S SPOTLESS, TACKY NOUVEAU RICHE LIVING ROOM IN CHILDRESS, TEXAS: 1982:

LUREEN, almost forty now, hair stiffly styled and even bigger, bleached-blond hair, makeup even thicker, business-like, cold, direct, answers the telephone.

LUREEN
Hello?

ENNIS
Uh, hello, this is Ennis del Mar, I, uh....

(CONTINUED)

CONTINUED:

LUREEN
Who? Who is this?

ENNIS
Ennis del Mar. I'm an old buddy of Jack's, I....

LUREEN
(interrupts, speaks quickly, allows no interruptions)
Jack used to mention you. You're the fishing buddy or the hunting buddy, I know that. Would have let you know, but wasn't sure about your name or address. Jack kept his friends' addresses in his head.

ENNIS
Why I was callin', to see what happened....

LUREEN
(level voice)
Oh yeah, Jack was pumping up a flat on the truck out on a back road when the tire blew up. The rim of the tire slammed into his face and broke his nose and jaw, knocked him unconscious on his back. By the time somebody came along, he had drowned in his own blood. Terrible thing. He was only thirty-nine years old.

EXT: RIVERTON, WYOMING: PAY TELEPHONE: DAY: CONTINUOUS: 1982:

WE'VE left LUREEN, and the screen holds only ENNIS.

ENNIS can't answer right away. He wonders, suddenly, if it was the tire iron:

SHARP CUT TO

ENNIS'S POV: MIDDLE OF NOWHERE: DUSK: CONTINUOUS: 1982:

A FLASH--JUST A SECOND OR TWO--ENNIS and WE SEE, in the evening shadows, a MAN being beaten unmercifully by THREE ASSAILANTS, one of whom uses a tire iron.

SHARP CUT BACK TO

EXT: RIVERTON, WYOMING: PAY TELEPHONE: DAY: CONTINUOUS: 1982:

The huge sadness of the northern plains rolls down upon ENNIS. He doesn't know which way it was, the tire iron--or a real accident, blood choking down JACK'S throat and nobody to turn him over.

The wind drones.

LUREEN
(not sure he's still there)
...Hello?

ENNIS
He buried down there?

LUREEN
We put a stone up. He was cremated, like he wanted, and half his ashes was interred here. The rest I sent up with his folks. He use to say he wanted his ashes scattered on Brokeback Mountain, but I wasn't sure where that was. I thought Brokeback Mountain might be around where he grew up. But knowing Jack, it might be some pretend place where the bluebirds sing and there's a whiskey spring.

ENNIS can hardly speak.

ENNIS
...No, ma'am, we herded sheep up on Brokeback one summer....

LUREEN
Well, he said it was his favorite place. I thought he meant to get drunk. He drank a lot.

ENNIS
His folks still up in Lightnin' Flat?

LUREEN
They'll be there till the day they die.

ENNIS
Thanks for your time, then...I sure am sorry...we was good friends....

(CONTINUED)

CONTINUED:

LUREEN
Get in touch with his folks. I suppose they'd appreciate it if his wishes was carried out. About the ashes, I mean.

Although she is polite, her little voice is as cold as ice.

ENNIS hangs up.

Looks like death.

EXT: OUTSIDE OF LIGHTNING FLAT, WYOMING: TWIST HOMESTEAD: HOUSE: FRONT PORCH: DAY: 1982:

ENNIS pulls his pickup truck up in front of the TWIST house.

Stops.

A rather thin woman--probably sixty to sixty-five--comes out the door and on to the front porch that stretches across the front of a tiny windbeaten house, four rooms, two down, two up: this is JACK'S childhood home, and this is JACK'S MOTHER. Shades her eyes as she squints, looking at the pickup truck.

EXT: OUTSIDE OF LIGHTNING FLAT, WYOMING: TWIST HOMESTEAD: HOUSE: DAY: CONTINUOUS: 1982:

Gets out. Tips his hat to JACK'S MOTHER.

INT: OUTSIDE OF LIGHTNING FLAT, WYOMING: TWIST HOMESTEAD: HOUSE: KITCHEN: DAY: 1982:

ENNIS sits at the little kitchen table with JACK'S parents.

Across from him sits JACK'S father, his hands folded on the plastic tablecloth. The father is tough, weatherbeaten, testy, critical--makes it clear by his manner that he expects to be stud duck in the pond.

JACK'S MOTHER--silent, defeated--stands.

ENNIS can't see JACK in either of them.

JACK'S MOTHER
(a polite shell of a woman)
Want a cup a coffee, don't you? Piece of cherry cake?

ENNIS
(stiff but polite)
Thank you, ma'am. I'll take a cup a coffee, but I can't eat no cake just now.

(CONTINUED)

CONTINUED:

JOHN TWIST stares at ENNIS with an angry, knowing expression.

ENNIS (CONT'D)
I feel awful bad about Jack...can't begin to tell you how bad I feel. I knew him a long time.
(pause)
I come by to say that if you want me to take his ashes up there on Brokeback like his wife said he wanted, I'd be proud to.

There is an uncomfortable silence.

ENNIS clears his throat, but then says nothing.

JOHN TWIST
Tell you what. I know where Brokeback Mountain is. He thought he was too goddamn special to be buried in the family plot.

JACK'S MOTHER--never a part of her husband's life--endures this.

JOHN TWIST (CONT'D)
(angrily)
Jack used a say, 'Ennis del Mar,' he used a say, 'I'm goin' a bring him up here one a these days and we'll lick this damn ranch into shape.' He had some half-baked notion the two a you was goin' a move up here, build a cabin, help run the place.
(pause)
Then this spring he's got another fella's goin' a come up here with him and build a place and help run the ranch, some ranch neighbor a his from down in Texas. He's goin' a split up with his wife and come back here.
(sarcastic)
So he says. But like most a Jack's ideas it never come to pass.

WE SEE the color drain from ENNIS'S face.

A beat.

JACK'S MOTHER
I kept his room like it was when he was a boy. I think he appreciated that.
(pause)
(MORE)

(CONTINUED)

CONTINUED: (2)

JACK'S MOTHER (CONT'D)
You are welcome to go up in his room, if you want.

ENNIS stands, wanting to be anywhere but here, in this kitchen, with JOHN TWIST.

ENNIS
I'd like that, ma'am, thank you.

INT: OUTSIDE LIGHTNING FLAT, WYOMING: TWIST HOMESTEAD: HOUSE: TOP OF STAIRS: JACK'S ROOM: DAY: CONTINUOUS: 1982:

WE SEE ENNIS climb a narrow set of stairs. Enters JACK'S room, tiny and hot, afternoon sun pouring through the west window, hitting the narrow boy's bed against the wall.

A well-used desk and a wooden chair stand against the other wall. A small .22 hangs in a wooden rack over the bed.

A window looks down on the dirt road stretching south...the only road out of this godforsaken place. ENNIS goes to the window. Opens it.

Sits for a moment, looking out at the bleak plain.

Turns, looks around the room.

ENNIS sees the closet. Gets up, walks over to it.

A shallow cavity with a wooden rod braced across it, a faded cretonne curtain on a string half-open, closing the closet off from the rest of the room. In the closet hangs two pairs of jeans crease-ironed and folded neatly over wire hangers. On the floor a pair of worn packer boots.

ENNIS looks inside to the left, and WE SEE that the closet makes a tiny jog into the wall--a little hiding place--and there, stiff with long suspension from a nail, hangs a shirt.

ENNIS lifts its sleeve: it's JACK'S old shirt from Brokeback days, dried blood on the sleeve, ENNIS'S own blood, from their last day together on Brokeback, when they were wrestling and ENNIS slipped and JACK accidentally kneed him in the nose.

The shirt seems heavy. Then ENNIS sees that there is another shirt inside it, the sleeves carefully worked down inside JACK'S shirt sleeves: it is ENNIS'S own shirt, lost, he'd thought, long ago up on Brokeback Mountain, his dirty shirt, the pocket ripped, buttons missing, stolen by JACK and hidden here inside JACK'S own shirt, the pair like two skins, one inside the other, two in one.

(CONTINUED)

CONTINUED:

ENNIS presses his face into the fabric and breathes in slowly through his mouth, hoping for the faintest smoke and mountain sage and salty sweet stink of JACK.

But there is no real scent, only the memory of it, the imagined power of Brokeback Mountain, of which nothing is left but what he now holds in his trembling hands.

INT: OUTSIDE LIGHTNING FLAT, WYOMING: TWIST HOMESTEAD: HOUSE: KITCHEN: DAY: 1982:

ENNIS is back downstairs, his hat in his hand, standing in the kitchen.

JACK'S MOTHER places the two shirts in a paper sack for ENNIS.

JOHN TWIST still sits at the table, stiff and angry as ever.

JOHN TWIST
Tell you what, we got a family plot and he's goin' in it.

ENNIS, resigned to this fact, nods at the old man as if he understands.

ENNIS
Yes sir.

JACK'S MOTHER hands him the sack with the two shirts.

JACK'S MOTHER
(sympathetic)
You come back and see us again.

ENNIS
(nods )
Ma'am. Thank you for this.

ENNIS puts his hat on.

Leaves.

EXT: OUTSIDE LIGHTNING FLAT, WYOMING: TWIST HOMESTEAD: YARD: DAY: 1982:

ENNIS looks back at the house, up at the window to JACK'S room.

Turns, stands in the little yard a moment looking off, nothing between the lonely house and the far horizon.

EXT: OUTSIDE LIGHTNING FLAT, WYOMING: TWIST HOMESTEAD: DIRT DRIVEWAY: DAY: 1982:

ENNIS is in his pickup, bumping down the washboard road.

EXT: RIVERTON, WYOMING: DEL MAR TRAILER HOUSE: AFTERNOON: 1984:

The wind, as ever, blows.

ENNIS'S modest little trailer house, his battered pickup parked in front.

A new mailbox on the trailer house just to the right of the front door. ENNIS has a set of stick-on numbers in his hand. Peels the 1 off and precisely applies it, then the 7: 17.

Steps back, admires his work.

WE SEE a 1982 Chevy Camaro pull into his driveway behind his truck.

Engine cuts. ALMA JR. steps out of the Camaro and closes the door.

ENNIS smiles.

ALMA JR. walks up to her father.

ENNIS
Hey there, Junior....

ALMA JR.
Hey Daddy....

An awkward ENNIS gives his oldest daughter a hug. ALMA JR. returns her daddy's embrace--she clearly loves him.

ALMA JR. (CONT'D)
Like the car?

ENNIS nods.

ENNIS
Is it yours?

ALMA JR.
It's Kurt's.

ENNIS
(confused)
Thought you was seein' Troy.

(CONTINUED)

CONTINUED:

ALMA JR.
Troy?
(rolls her eyes)
Daddy, that was two years ago.

A beat.

ENNIS
Troy still playin' baseball?

ALMA JR.
Don't know what he's doin'. I'm seein' Kurt now.

ENNIS
What's this Kurt fella do?

ALMA JR.
Works out in the oil fields.

ENNIS
(nods)
Roughneck.
(beat)
You're nineteen, guess you can do whatever you want.

ENNIS opens the door to his trailer and holds it for ALMA JR. They enter the trailer. The door slams loudly.

INT: RIVERTON, WYOMING: DEL MAR TRAILER HOUSE: AFTERNOON: CONTINUOUS: 1984:

ALMA JR. sits on a ragged couch.

ENNIS stands and pours her a cup of coffee from a stained Mr. Coffee. WE HEAR wind blowing, rattling the trailer house.

ALMA JR. looks around the nearly empty trailer, an homage to plains-life minimalism: a TV sits on a plastic milk crate in front of a battered recliner, the only other furniture besides the chipped Formica table, two wobbly chairs, and a fridge and tiny stove.

ALMA JR.
(makes her sad)
Daddy, you need more furniture.

ENNIS fits the coffeepot back into the Mr. Coffee machine.

ENNIS
(looking around the empty trailer)
(MORE)

(CONTINUED)

CONTINUED:

ENNIS (CONT'D)
If you don't got nothin', then you don't need nothin'.

ENNIS sits down across from her.

ENNIS (CONT'D)
So what's the occasion?

ALMA JR. blows on her coffee, something on her mind. This is hard for her....

ALMA JR.
(apprehensive)
Me and Kurt...we're getting married.

Looks at his oldest daughter.

ENNIS
How long you known this Kurt fella?

ALMA JR.
(relieved, talks faster)
About a year. Wedding'll be June fifth at the Methodist Church. Jenny's singing, and Monroe's gonna cater the reception.

A beat.

ENNIS
This Kurt fella...does he love you?

ALMA JR. is startled--and touched--by the question.

ALMA JR.
Yes, Daddy. He loves me.

ENNIS nods, almost as if to himself.

ALMA JR. (CONT'D)
(pause)
Was hoping you'd be there, Daddy.

ENNIS
Supposed to be on a roundup over near the Tetons....

Something sags a little in ALMA JR. Nods her head. Understands.

ENNIS looks across at his daughter. Sees her disappointment.

He stands. Goes to the fridge, opens it. Takes out a half-empty bottle of cheap white wine, a legacy of CASSIE.

(CONTINUED)

CONTINUED: (2)

ENNIS (CONT'D))
(smiles at his daughter)
You know what? I reckon they can find themselves another cowboy.

Takes two jelly glasses from the dry rack next to the sink, unscrews the bottle top, fills both.

ENNIS (CONT'D)
My little girl...is gettin' married.

Hands her a glass of wine. Sits.

ENNIS (CONT'D)
(raising his glass)
To Alma and Kurt.

ALMA JR. smiles, and clinks her glass with her daddy's.

ENNIS smiles back at his luminous daughter. But his smile can't hide his regret and longing, for the one thing that he can't have. That he will never have.

EXT: RIVERTON, WYOMING: DEL MAR TRAILER HOUSE: AFTERNOON: FEW MINUTES LATER: 1984:

ENNIS stands outside.

ALMA JR., in Kurt's Camaro, backs out and drives off, waving to her father as she goes.

ENNIS waves back, until she's well down the road.

Turns.

Goes back inside his crumpled little trailer house.

INT: RIVERTON, WYOMING: DEL MAR TRAILER HOUSE: DAY: CONTINUOUS: 1984:

ENNIS, back inside now, notices that ALMA JR. has left her sweater hanging over her chair.

He picks it up, hurries back to the door, opens it.

Sees she's long gone.

Folds the sweater. Goes to a little closet, opens the door. He places ALMA JR.'s sweater on the top shelf of the closet.

And there, on the back of the closet door, WE SEE THE SHIRTS, on a wire hangar suspended from a nail, and next to them, a postcard of Brokeback Mountain, tacked onto the door.

(CONTINUED)

CONTINUED:

He has taken his shirt from inside of JACK'S, and has carefully tucked JACK'S shirt down inside his own.

He snaps the top button of one of the shirts.

Looks at the ensemble through a few stinging tears.

ENNIS
Jack, I swear....

Stands there for a moment.

Then closes the closet door.

He looks out the window, at the great bleakness of the vast northern plains....

THE END

# Getting Movied

## Annie Proulx

As a student of history and a writer of fiction my interest has focused on social and economic change in rural communities—Vermont, Newfoundland, Texas, Wyoming. I am something of a geographic determinist, believing that regional landscapes, climate and topography dictate local cultural traditions and kinds of work, and thereby the events on which my stories are built. Landscape is central to this rural fiction. I have been interested in the disappearance of dairy hill farms in New England, the collapsing fishing industry in Atlantic Canada and the slow fade of cattle ranching in the west.

*Close Range* contains nine stories, including "Brokeback Mountain," ostensibly concerned with Wyoming landscape and making a living in hard, isolated livestock-raising communities dominated by white masculine values, but also holding subliminal fantasies. Most of the stories are loosely based on historical events, as the botched castration in "People in Hell Just Want a Drink of Water." "Brokeback" was not connected to any one incident, but based on a coalescence of observations over many years, small things here and there.

Sometime in early 1997 the story took shape. One night in a bar upstate I had noticed an older ranch hand, maybe in his late sixties, obviously short on the world's luxury goods. Although spruced up for Friday night his clothes were a little ragged, boots stained and worn. I had seen him around, working cows, helping with sheep, taking orders from a ranch manager. He was thin and lean, muscular in a stringy kind of way. He leaned against the back wall and his eyes were fastened not on the dozens of handsome and flashing women in the room but on the young cowboys playing pool. Maybe he was following the game, maybe he knew the players, maybe one was his son or nephew, but there was something in his expression, a kind of bitter longing, that made me wonder if he was country gay. Then I began to consider what it might have been like for him—not the real person against the wall, but for any ill-informed, confused, not-sure-of-what-he-was-feeling youth growing up in homophobic rural Wyoming. A few weeks later I listened to the vicious rant of an elderly bar-café owner who was incensed that two "homos" had come in the night before and ordered dinner. She said that if her bar regulars had been there (it was darts tournament night) things would have gone badly for them. "Brokeback" was constructed on the small but tight idea of a couple of home-grown country kids, opinions and self-knowledge shaped by the world around them, finding themselves in emotional waters of increasing depth. I wanted to develop the story through a kind of literary *sostenente*.

The early sixties seemed the right time period. The two characters had to have grown up on isolated hardscrabble ranches and were clearly homophobic themselves, especially the Ennis character. Both wanted to be cowboys, be part of the Great Western Myth, but it didn't work out that way; Ennis never got to be more than a rough-cut ranch hand and Jack Twist chose rodeo as an expression of cowboy. Neither of them was ever a top hand, and they met herding sheep, animals most real cowpokes despise. Although they were not really cowboys (the word "cowboy" is often used derisively in the west by those who do ranch work), the urban critics dubbed it a tale of two gay cowboys. No. It is a story of destructive rural homophobia. Although there are many places in Wyoming where gay men did and do live together in harmony with the community, it should not be forgotten that a year after this story was published Matthew Shepard was tied to a buck fence outside the most enlightened town in the state, Laramie, home of the University of Wyoming. Note, too, the fact that

Wyoming has the highest suicide rate in the country, and that the preponderance of those people who kill themselves are elderly single men.

In my mind isolation and altitude—the fictional Brokeback Mountain, a place both empowering and inimical—began to shape the story. The mountain had to force everything that happened to these two young men. I have many times heard Wyomingites who have gone east for one reason or another talk about how badly they missed their natural terrain, the long sight lines, the clear thin air, how claustrophobic were trees and how dead the atmosphere without the constant flow of wind, and I find it so myself. It seemed to me that the story could only balance on love, something all humans need and give, whether to one's children, parents, or a lover of the opposite or same sex. I wanted to explore both long-lasting love and its possible steep price tag, both homophobic antipathy and denial. I knew this was a story loaded with taboos but I was driven to write it. These characters did something that, as a writer, I had never experienced before—they began to get very damn real. Usually I deal in obedient characters who do what they are told, but Jack and Ennis soon seemed more vivid than many of the flesh-and-blood people around me and there emerged an antiphonal back-and-forth relationship between writer and character. I've heard other writers mention this experience but it was the first time for me.

As I worked on the story over the next months scenes appeared and disappeared. (The story went through more than sixty revisions.) The mountain encounter had to be—shall we say?—"seminal" and brief. One spring, years before, I had been in the Big Horns and noticed distant flocks of sheep on great empty slopes. From the heights I had been able to see a hundred miles and more to the plains. In such isolated high country, away from opprobrious comment and watchful eyes, I thought it would be plausible for the characters to get into a sexual situation. That's nothing new or out of the ordinary; livestock workers have a blunt and full understanding of the sexual behaviors of man and beast. High lonesome situation, a couple of guys—expediency sometimes rules and nobody needs to talk about it and that's how it is. One old sheep rancher, dead now, used to say he always sent up two men to tend the sheep "so's if they get lonesome they can poke each other." From that perspective Aguirre, the hiring man, would have winked and said nothing, and Ennis's remark to Jack that this was a one-shot deal would have been accurate. The complicating factor was that they both fell into once-in-a-lifetime love. I strove to give Jack and Ennis depth and complexity and to mirror real life by rasping that love against the societal norms that both men obeyed, both of them marrying and begetting children, both loving their children, and, in a way, their wives.

Many gay men marry and have children and are good fathers. Because this is a rural story, family and children are important. Most stories (and many films) I have seen about gay relationships take place in urban settings and never have children in them. The rural gay men I know like kids, and if they don't have their own, they usually have nephews and nieces who claim a big place in their hearts. For both characters to marry women enlarges the story and introduces two young wives who move from innocence and happy trust to some pretty hard lessons about real life. Alma and Lureen give the story a universal connection, for men and women need each other, sometimes in unusual ways.

It was a hard story to write. Sometimes it took weeks to get the right phrase or descriptor for particular characters. I remember vividly that, driving on Owl Canyon Road in Colorado down over the state line one afternoon and thinking about Jack Twist's father, the expression "stud duck," which I had heard somewhere, came to me as the right way to succinctly describe that hard little man, and a curve in the road became the curve that killed Ennis's parents. The scene for the kiss when Jack and Ennis reunite after four years occurred in its entirety as I drove past the Laramie cement plant—so much for scenery. In fact I did most of the "writing" while I was driving. The most difficult scene was the paragraph where, on the mountain, Ennis holds Jack and rocks back and forth, humming, the moment mixed with childhood loss and his refusal to admit he was holding a man. This paragraph took forever to get right and I played Charlie Haden and Pat Metheny's "Spiritual" from their album *Beyond the*

*Missouri Sky (Short Stories)* uncountable times trying to get the words. I was trying to write the inchoate feelings of Jack and Ennis, the sad impossibility of their liaison, which for me was expressed in that music. To this day I cannot hear that track without Jack and Ennis appearing before me. The scraps that feed a story come from many cupboards.

I was an aging female writer, married too many times, and though I have a few gay friends, there were things I was not sure about. I talked with a sheep rancher to be sure that it was historically accurate to use a couple of white ranch kids as flock tenders in the early sixties, for I knew that in previous decades it had been mostly Basques who did this job, and today it is often men from the South American countries. But jobs were scarce in Wyoming in that period and even married couples with children got hired to herd sheep. One of my oldest friends, Tom Watkin, with whom I once published a rural newspaper, read and commented on the story as it developed. I thought too much about this story. It was supposed to be Ennis who had dreams about Jack but I had dreams about both of them. I still had little distance from it when it was published in *The New Yorker* on October 13, 1997. I expected letters from outraged religio-moral types, but instead got them from men, quite a few of them Wyoming ranch hands and cowboys and the fathers of men, who said "you told my story" or "I now understand what my son went through." I still, eight years later, get those heart-wrenching letters.

When I got Diana Ossana and Larry McMurtry's request to option the story for a film with money from their own pockets—unusual for screenwriters—I was immediately beset with doubts. I simply did not think this story could be a film: it was too sexually explicit for presumed mainstream tastes, the general topic of homophobia was a hot potato unless gingerly skirted, and, given Hollywood actors' reluctance to play gay men (though many gay men have brilliantly played straight guys) it would likely be difficult to find a good cast, not to say a director. It was only because I trusted Larry's and Diana's writing skills, film experience and, especially, Larry's incomparable knowledge of the west's mores and language that I signed the contract.

It didn't take them long. Within a few months I was reading their powerful screenplay constructed from the story, but richly augmenting it, adding new flesh to its long bones, filling out the personalities, introducing a little humor and new characters who moved the story along its close-set rails. Yes, the screenplay was beautiful, but my worries continued. What producers would be interested in a story about homophobic gay Wyoming ranch hands? What actors would have the guts to do this? What director would take the risk? How severely would the screenplay be clawed to pieces? The freedom-granting yet hostile landscape, of course, would be utterly lost, and with it, the literal grounding of the story. I thought the screenplay was as far as the movie would go, and I wasn't sorry.

Screenwriters almost always deal with adapting novels to film, and necessarily great chunks are excised, crunched, plots straitjacketed, dialogue transmuted into television-speak. This was different. Larry and Diana were working with a short story which came with a sturdy framework. But there was not enough there. I write in a tight, compressed style that needs air and loosening to unfold into art. They had to invent, enlarge and imagine. It was, in a real way, a collaboration. I began to wonder why movie people didn't prefer short stories to novels, since the opportunity for original work is built in.

Over the next few years several producers and directors appeared on the horizon, but there were problems with all of them. Larry liked an interesting young filmmaker who had made a funny and original short feature. I met this fellow in Tucson and liked him, hoped he would understand the place and the characters. We arranged to meet again in Wyoming so he could look at the terrain and possible scene sites. He came with a photographer, advisor, location person and others. That meeting turned into something I think of as "The Wyoming Death Trip." From the start, everywhere the tenderhearted city folk looked there was a dead animal. First it was deer by the side of the highway, then squashed rabbits on the tarmac. We stopped at a sheepherder's home quarters. He was out with the sheep, but as it was spring there was a makeshift pen with a few dozen bum lambs in it. One of the film entourage spied a dead lamb by the side of the fence and freaked. He decided (erroneously) that the lambs were starving to death, and, a man of action, rustled around until he found a bag of feed, poured some into a pan and set it in the pen. Keith, the ranch hand showing us around, blanched. I suggested we leave the lambs, hoping the sheepherder paid to look after them would not pursue us with a machete. We went to an untenanted house that might work as Ennis and Alma's place. But as soon as we stepped inside, there, near the hem of a long curtain that reached the floor, lay a dead mouse. We finished the day at a lonely ranch house outside Ucross called "the old Childress place." Empty for years, the crawl space below was a haven for rattlesnakes, the interior home for other animals needing shelter. We looked into a dusty room with a hole in the ceiling where once the stovepipe exited. The Los Angeles people sucked in their breaths as one, for on the floor lay the dried remains of a rabbit, discarded by an owl. That was it. These urban people just did not get it that Wyoming has a lot of wildlife and that the wildlife sometimes gets dead. Animals and rural places were clearly alien to them, and just as clearly I knew they could not make this film. And I pretty much gave up on the whole idea. It wasn't going to happen, because there were no producers or directors who understood the rural west, the rural anything. Old story.

A long time later Focus Films showed interest. That was encouraging, as they, in an earlier incarnation known as Good Machine, had produced the successful film version of *The Laramie Project*. I had met one of the people involved with that film in Denver one night, and we had gone up the street looking for a CD of Jim White's "Wrong-Eyed Jesus," which was a great favorite of mine at that time. So I was inclined toward Focus. They were suggesting Ang Lee as the director, and I thought, here we go again. Could a Taiwanese-born director, probably a thoroughgoing urbanite, who had recently re-created *The Hulk,* understand Wyoming and the subterranean forces of the place? I doubted it. But the wheels were rolling now. I didn't know what to expect and tried not to think about it.

On a New York visit I met James Schamus briefly, and Ang Lee in a funky boîte far downtown. I was nervous about meeting Ang Lee despite his reputation as brilliant and highly skilled. Would we have anything to say to each other? Were the cultural gaps surmountable? We smiled and made small talk for a while and then, reassured by something in his quietness, I said that I was very afraid about this story, that making stories sometimes took me into off-limits places and that I feared the film would not follow that path. He said that he was afraid, too, that it would be extremely difficult to make into a film. He said he had recently lost his father. I remembered from my mother's death a few years earlier the vast hole in the world that opened and could not be pulled closed. I had a glimmering that Ang Lee might use his sorrow creatively, transferring a personal sense of loss to this film about two men for whom things cannot work out, that he might be able to show the grief and anger that builds when we must accept severe emotional wounding. I felt we both knew that this story was risky and that he wanted to take the story on, probably for the creative challenge and perhaps (though he didn't say so) for the gasping euphoria when you get into unknown but hard-driving imaginative projects. However slender, there was a positive connection.

Later there were some disagreements. In the written story the motel scene after a four-year hiatus stood as central. During their few hours in the Motel Siesta, Jack's and Ennis's paths were irrevocably laid out. In the film that Ang Lee already had shaped in his mind, the emotional surge contained in that scene would be better shifted to a later point and melded with the men's painful last meeting. I didn't understand this until I saw the film in September 2005 and recognized the power of this timing. Although I have always known that films and books have different rises and falls, different shapes, it's easier to know that in the abstract than on the killing ground. At some point I wrote a letter pleading for the motel scene that went for naught. It was out of my hands, no longer my story, but Ang Lee's film. And so I said goodbye to Jack and Ennis and got on with other work.

Before I finally saw the film I had heard from Larry and Diana that it was very good, that the language was intact, that the actors were superb. But I was not prepared for the emotional hammering I got when I saw it. The characters roared back into my mind, larger and stronger than they had ever been. Here it was, the point that writers do not like to admit; in our time film can be more powerful than the written word. I realized that if Ang Lee had been born in Barrow or Novosibirsk it would likely have been the same. He understands human feelings and is not afraid to walk into dangerous territory.

Seeing the film disturbed me. I felt that, as the ancient Egyptians had removed a corpse's brain through the nostril with a slender hook before mummification, the cast and crew of this film, from the director down, had gotten into my mind and pulled out images. Especially did I feel this about Heath Ledger, who knew better than I how Ennis felt and thought, whose intimate depiction of that achingly needy ranch kid builds with frightening power. It is an eerie sensation to see events you have imagined in the privacy of your mind, and tried hopelessly to transmit to others through little black marks on a page, loom up before you in an overwhelming visual experience. I realized that I, as a writer, was having the rarest film trip: my story was not mangled but enlarged into huge and gripping imagery that rattled minds and squeezed hearts.

The film is intensely Wyoming. Lee included dead animals and good fights, both very western. Although it was shot mostly in Alberta, production designer Judy Becker toured Texas and Wyoming, noting landforms and long views. A few weeks after I saw it for the first time I was driving through the Sierra Madre. It was a windless, brilliant day, the aspen lit by slant-handed autumnal light; hunting season and time for the annual shove-down, when stockmen with Forest Service allowances move their cows and sheep to the lower slopes before the early storms. As I came around a corner I had to stop to let a band of sheep cross the highway. In the trees on the upslope stood a saddled horse, bedroll tied on behind, rifle in scabbard; behind it stood a laden pack horse. No rider in sight. I thought I would wait a minute and see if Jack or Ennis might come out of the trees; then I shook my head, feeling wacky to have tangled the film and reality, and pretty sure that neither character was going to show.

Aside from the two-faced landscape, aside from the virtuoso acting, aside from the stunning and subtle makeup job of aging these two young men twenty years, an accumulation of very small details gives the film authenticity and authority: Ennis's dirty fingernails in a love scene, the old highway sign ENTERING WYOMING not seen here for decades, the slight paunch Jack develops as he ages, the splotch of nail polish on Lureen's finger in the painful telephone scene, her mother's perfect Texas hair, Ennis and Jack sharing a joint instead of a cigarette in the 1970s, the switched-around shirts, the speckled enamel coffeepot, all accumulate and convince us of the truth of the story. People may doubt that young men fall in love up on the snowy heights, but no one disbelieves the speckled coffeepot, and if the coffeepot is true, so is the other.

# Adapting Brokeback Mountain

## Larry McMurtry

SOME THIRTY YEARS AGO, IN A COLUMN IN *AMERICAN FILM,* I POSED A question: Why do great works of literature so rarely get adapted into equally great films? Tolstoy's *Anna Karenina* has been filmed—not ineptly—several times, but the novel is immeasurably greater than any of the films.

In the column, I suggested several reasons why great writing gets treated—for the most part—so inadequately in films. For one thing, the knowledge that they are setting out to film a known masterpiece is likely to inhibit directors, to one degree or another. Then there is the problem of literary style, which, in great books, is often inseparable from the subject matter. Style and substance fuse so intricately that most directors will be hard put to find even an approximate cinematic equivalent to a literary style.

My own early picaresque novel, *All My Friends Are Going to Be Strangers,* is a case in point. The book has great appeal to filmmakers. It has been scripted more than a dozen times; several eminent directors have approached it, only to quickly back away. Why? Because somehow the fun—perhaps even the essence—of that novel is in the prose. How on earth would one render its absurdist, frolicsome qualities on the screen? To date, no director has dared to take the leap.

In my column, I argued that flat, rather plain-styled novels, such as my own *Last Picture Show,* are usually better vehicles for adaptation than towering masterpieces. Of course, there will always be exceptions: the director George Stevens took Theodore Dreiser's plain-styled masterpiece *An American Tragedy* and did it full justice in his own masterful film *A Place in the Sun*.

The exception to the strong book/weak film rule that means most to me and to my writing partner Diana Ossana is, of course, Annie Proulx's great short story "Brokeback Mountain," which has now been filmed—wonderfully—by Ang Lee. As adapters, we did our level best to follow the clear track of the story, augmenting and amplifying, adding texture and substance where necessary. Both Diana and I felt privileged during the entire endeavor: a literary masterpiece, but one accessible to the screenwriters and filmmakers, had come our way. What was there to do but be glad?

Though "Brokeback Mountain" is surely a masterpiece, it is also—fortunately for Ang—a very *young* masterpiece, less than ten years old, and, perhaps for that reason, less inhibiting to the director. The story of the long-frustrated love of Ennis del Mar and Jack Twist slots into the strong, long American tradition of doomed young men: *The Great Gatsby, The Sun Also Rises, Miss Lonelyhearts* and many others. Except when together, Ennis and Jack are very lonely young men. Though short in compass—only eleven pages in the *New Yorker* version—it echoes as powerfully as a high plains thunderclap.

I was the more stunned when I read "Brokeback Mountain" because I realized that it was a story that had been sitting there all my life, fifty-five years of which have been lived in the American West. There the story was, all those years, waiting in patient distance for someone to write it.

Now Annie Proulx has written it, in spare, wire-fence prose that is congruent with the landscape itself, and with the struggling, bruised speech still to be heard today across the north plains.

* * *

I have written elsewhere that the dominant visual mode of dealing with the American West, from the day the first painter set foot west of the Mississippi, has been lyrical pastoralism. Just find a mountain range, with a river running through it, and the cloak of pastoralism is there, either to protect you or smother you, as the case may be. Ang Lee is a reluctant, even an unwilling, pastoralist. He gets as much of the grit of the towns as he can into the picture, but since it is to the mountains that the two lovers go for their brief reunions, the landscape itself poeticizes their union more than the director would have probably liked. John Ford addressed this problem by making Monument Valley stand for the whole West—if he had to have a hill, he would make it a red butte, and the fact that Monument Valley is a landscape unique in the world did not deter him.

The photographic image that best illustrates the poeticizing strength of American West pastoralism is Ansel Adams's *Moonrise, Hernandez, New Mexico,* in which a huge, splendid full moon rises over what appears to be a humble hamlet in New Mexico. But—one must ask—what about the people who live possibly ragged lives beneath that glorious moon? To see what the West has done to the people who live with its harshness as well as its beauty, you need to go not to the pastoralists, but—as Diana Ossana also suggests—to Richard Avedon's great *In the American West,* a book of extraordinary photographs just now being reexhibited, in all their life-size starkness, at the Amon Carter Museum in Fort Worth, Texas.

The West of the great mountains, of the high plains and rippling rivers, is very beautiful, so beautiful that it tempts many not to see, or want to see, the harshness of the lives of the people who live in the bleak little towns and have to brush the grit of the plains off their teeth at night.

Richard Avedon realized, as did Ang Lee in his turn, how seductive Western landscape can be. Who would not be seduced by that great moon rising over that crumbling village? Then, if you look a little farther west, there will always be the Tetons, and you are in the world of *Shane,* itself a story of loss and sorrow. Richard Avedon eliminated pastoralism altogether by shooting all of his subjects against a white paper background.

Ang Lee did not have that option, but he was well aware of the pastoralist danger when he came to film *Brokeback Mountain:* look too often at those hills, lie too long beside those rippling rivers, and you may think you are hearing a love song, when actually it is a death song.

*Brokeback Mountain* is a tragedy of emotional deprivation, as not a few western stories are, and the fact that Ennis and Jack and their families so often find themselves heartbroken in beautiful country only makes the heartbreak worse.

# Climbing Brokeback Mountain

## Diana Ossana

READING HAS BEEN THE ONE CONSTANT IN MY LIFE, AND MORE OFTEN than not a refuge: from chores; from people; from hardships of various kinds; from the random perversity of life; but mostly, from insomnia.

Insomnia has been a lifelong affliction, in that I'm incapable of sleeping more than four hours at a stretch. Reading in the middle of the night can be an indulgence, since there are minimal distractions: long periods with no parental squabbles, no younger siblings to tend or to torment me, no telephones to answer, no neighbors coming to the door, no work to start or finish. It was easy to become fully absorbed in whatever story I happened to be reading at the time, and to become one—or all—of the characters, to again experience feelings I had already felt or to live lives I might never have had the opportunity to know otherwise. Reading fiction is especially liberating for someone who struggles with expressing normal human emotion or who spends the majority of day-to-day life simply trying to get by.

So it happened that in the fall of 1997, while living in Larry McMurtry's prairie-style home in Archer City, Texas, in the middle of a long, sleepless night, I picked up the October 13 issue of *The New Yorker* and began reading Annie Proulx's "Brokeback Mountain."

I was seduced by the simple lyricism of Annie's prose and then startled by its rawness and power. By the time I reached the last words of the story, I felt, to paraphrase Annie's own words, as if my guts had been pulled out hand over hand a yard at a time. This spare narrative about a doomed love between two unremarkable men tapped deep into my own private well of pain and regret, and I was weeping by the end, deep, gut-wrenching sobs. I got up, splashed water on my face, lay back down and fell asleep.

When I awoke the next morning, my first thought was that my epiphany had been a fluke, one of those middle-of-the-night obsessive realizations that might never feel as meaningful in the light of day. I had to reread "Brokeback."

That first reading was about the tragedy of Ennis del Mar, clenched and terrified, incapable of imagining a life different than the one he had chosen for himself. The second reading revealed to me more layers of tragedy—Jack's wretched, unrequited love; Alma's fragmented hopes and quiet despair; Lureen's cumulative bitterness. I felt broken in two.

I sensed immediately that this was a great story with the power to touch many people. I felt it ought to be out in the world in some major, major way. I knew then that I wanted to adapt "Brokeback Mountain" into a screenplay. I hurried downstairs to find Larry. He had just returned from his bookstore, and I cornered him in the kitchen.

Would you please read this short story?

No. You know I don't read short fiction anymore.

I know, I know. Just humor me.

My abrupt tone must have spurred him, because he took the magazine upstairs, came back down in fifteen minutes and admitted it was the best short story he'd ever read in *The New Yorker*. I asked him if he thought we could adapt it into a screenplay. He considered for a moment, and agreed we could. We sat down, wrote Annie Proulx a single-page letter and put it in the mail. I phoned our manager at the time and explained that we wanted to option and adapt a short story for film. It was a tragedy about two poor Wyoming ranch hands who fall in love in 1963, I said, and he told me to forget it—just forget it—because it would never get made. I recalled D. H. Lawrence's "never trust the teller, trust the tale," and I said please, just read the story. By the end of the day, he was back on the phone, urging us to write to the author immediately—which, of course, we had already done.

That evening, I asked Larry how he would feel if any staunch *Lonesome Dove* fans turned against him for being involved with a film that subverts the myth of the American West and its iconic heroes. He replied that he'd never given it a thought. I told him good, I figured as much, I just needed to hear you say the words. That was the only time we ever spoke about any political implications to making a film of "Brokeback Mountain."

Annie replied to our letter in less than a week. We optioned her story with our own money and promptly set about writing *Brokeback Mountain: A Screenplay,* Based on a Short Story by Annie Proulx.

Some time before I discovered "Brokeback Mountain," I had read and was deeply affected by Charles Frazier's luminous, heart-stopping novel *Cold Mountain*. *Cold Mountain* covers a short period of time near the end of the Civil War, but it is long, and dense with information. Larry and I are practical and unsentimental when adapting, and fairly adept at cutting a path through thickets of prose in order to shape a powerful screenplay, while maintaining the essence of character and story. We wanted to option and adapt Mr. Frazier's fine novel. It would have been a satisfying project, and one we could have enjoyed. But *Cold Mountain* quickly became a best-selling literary success, and the film rights slipped away for much more than two modest screenwriters could afford.

I mention this in order to point out some differences in adapting screenplays from novels and in adapting screenplays from short stories. *Cold Mountain* is 356 pages long. It covers a relatively short period of time, but it is detailed and full, with many characters and smaller stories contained within a larger story. I liken it to Homer's *Odyssey:* adventure after adventure confronts the hero, Inman, on his journey home from the Civil War. Imaginatively, the screenplay was nearly all contained within the novel. We would have had to be brutally economic, as concerned with carving away content as with creating structure.

## Diana Ossana

"Brokeback Mountain" is the final story in Annie Proulx's collection *Close Range: Wyoming Stories*. Its compelling narrative covers a substantial time period—twenty years—in thirty pages. The prose is tight, precise, spare, evocative, unsentimental and yet incredibly moving. The dialogue is specific to the time, the place, the social and economic class of the characters. It is a near perfect short story, in technique as well as emotion. And in my mind, it was an excellent blueprint for a screenplay. We could afford to option it with our own money. We did not have to streamline or condense. We had the luxury of using our own imaginations to expand and build upon that blueprint, rounding out characters, creating new scenes, fleshing out existing ones. It was such an enjoyable experience, it made me wonder why more short stories were not adapted into films.

We had a finished screenplay in three months, and sent it off to Wyoming. In a few days Annie phoned, and we spoke for over two hours. She had points she wanted to clarify, and a few corrections, but on the whole she seemed genuinely pleased with our work. I felt fortunate to have her input, because these people were born in her imagination. She and I spoke about Ennis and his stoicism, his background, his homophobic worldview, his inability to access his emotions. She talked a lot about Wyoming, its landscape, its people and their hardscrabble lives.

What she said to me in those two hours I mentally filed away. I referred back to it for the next eight years.

We sent the script to our representatives, who in turn sent it out into the world. Our *Brokeback Mountain* screenplay had been in existence for a year when young Matthew Shepard was brutally murdered in Laramie, Wyoming. It was horrifying. It felt like an eerie mirroring of Annie's story and our screenplay. My daughter, Sara, was attending the University of Wyoming in Laramie on a basketball scholarship when they found Matthew's body tied to a fence not five minutes from her apartment. I flew to Wyoming to be with her. While I was there, we went to visit Annie at her home in Centennial. We spent the day together, and she took us on a picnic up near the Medicine Bow. Annie was warm and welcoming, a strong, solid presence, and it was reassuring to Sara (and to me) to know she would be close by.

Larry and I continued on with our lives, such as they were, and took on work for hire, wrote screenplays and fiction. But *Brokeback Mountain* was still in the back of his mind, and in the front of mine. It was Larry's firm conviction that ours was an excellent screenplay, and to his way of thinking, good work will always find its way. He is a person who does not worry about much of anything, and I am a person who worries about most everything. (By now *Brokeback* had acquired the reductive and spurious Hollywood tagline "a story about gay cowboys," much as *Lonesome Dove* had been dubbed "a story about a cattle drive.") Over the years, many people tried to help make the film, but it never came together. None of us imagined it would take as long as it did to find partners with the courage and passion sufficient to commit to our risky but potentially groundbreaking project—but we never doubted we could find them.

One morning I got a phone call from a producer in Los Angeles, Michael Costigan. He had been reluctant to read the screenplay, he explained, since for years he had heard it described as "that gay cowboy script." But the night before he called, he had read it and was stunned by it. Then his girlfriend read it, and she was devastated by it. It was the best script either of them had ever read, he added. I told Michael if he wanted to be involved, there was no money to be had unless we could manage to get it made. He came on board anyway, and we soon became fast friends.

In time, we were fortunate in joining forces with Focus Features, whose copresident, James Schamus, had tried some years back to help make the film when he was an independent producer. And Ang Lee was free to direct. We spoke to Annie, who was in agreement, so negotiations began. I would be a producer; Larry and Michael would be executive producers.

After nearly seven years, *Brokeback Mountain* went into production in and around Calgary, Alberta, in late spring of 2004.

* * *

Film is a collaborative medium. Fiction writing, for the most part, is not. Making a film is like cooking: when all the ingredients are in proper balance, a dish can be ambrosial, but if the proportions are out of kilter, it can wind up a mess.

It is hard work to make any film, to make *every* film. It takes as much hard work to make a bad film as it does to make a good one, and so I was afraid of failure, too, that a film would not do justice to the story, that somehow between writing the script and making a film, it would be botched beyond recognition. And yet I never once lost faith in the potential of *Brokeback Mountain*.

If someone were to ask me why Ang Lee decided to film *Brokeback Mountain,* I would say that he is intelligent, perceptive—and a risk taker. Maybe those before him were too afraid of the powerful emotions evoked by the screenplay. Maybe they were afraid of being associated with a dramatic love story involving two men who were not hairdressers or drag queens. Or maybe they were simply afraid of failing. Whenever a person sets out on a creative endeavor, whether a poem, a short story, a novel, a screenplay or a film, that person risks failure. It takes someone brave—and maybe a bit foolhardy—to take that leap. But the exhilaration that comes from achievement—in writing a singular poem, a compelling short story, a convincing novel, in constructing a potent screenplay or in making an excellent film—far outweighs any risk.

Once Ang Lee committed to direct and Focus Features obtained financing, we cast the film in short order. Each role, in Larry's words, was cast "to perfection." I had long wanted Heath Ledger for our film, knew in my gut that he had it in him to portray Ennis. Larry saw only his performance in *Monster's Ball,* and with his keen eye and decisive manner remarked, "That young man *is* Ennis."

Collaboration, as I mention above, is the key word in filmmaking. Larry and I always remain receptive to suggestions regarding scene changes or structural shifts within a script. We saw our script as a long, honest and credible extension of Annie's writing, her dialogue, sense of time, place and landscape, but also remained open to scene and dialogue adjustments if they served the story and the characters.

Ang and the studio surrounded us with a brilliant crew, experienced, talented people who had worked with notables such as Martin Scorsese, Milos Forman, Stanley Kubrick, Robert Altman, David Cronenberg, Andy Warhol, Sergio Leone, Oliver Stone and Jim Jarmusch. They were from all over the world: North America, Taiwan, Australia, Mexico, South America, England, Italy. Most days I would look around and feel humbled by the talent our screenplay had managed to attract. Who was luckier than I?

*Brokeback Mountain* was filmed on a tight, modest budget. Every penny went toward production values. Larry and I were also lucky to be able to involve our children. My daughter, Sara, worked for five months in preproduction and throughout filming as an unpaid intern and assistant to Judy Becker, our knowledgeable and meticulous production designer, an invaluable experience for her. James McMurtry, Larry's gifted singer-songwriter son, wrote the words and music to "Water Walking Jesus," along with his good friend Stephen Bruton.

Michael Costigan was on set with us for nearly the entire shoot. His humor and innate common sense served us all in good stead. As the days passed and together we endured rain, snow, sleet, hail, sunburn, windburn, sheep wrangling, mosquitoes, flat tires, camping out, exhaustion, answering calls of nature wherever we could find cover and four-wheeling to the remotest of remote locations, we soon came to feel like a large extended family. And like family members who live and work in such close proximity, we had our share of squabbles, but mostly we got along, and I felt happy to be working with fine people who each expressed to me how passionate they felt about the screenplay and story, and how important it was to them to make a great film.

I carried a copy of Annie's short story with me every day on set while producing the film. Larry stayed in Tucson to write, and Annie stayed in Wyoming—but in spirit, they were with me throughout filming. Whenever I would feel exhausted or overwhelmed, I would center myself by rereading her story.

Another kind of talisman I kept close was a copy of Richard Avedon's unflinching photographic collection *In the American West*. I grew up in a working-class, Irish-Italian family in Missouri. A lot of our neighbors looked like the people on those pages. Avedon's stark, unromantic black-and-white images show men and women whose lives have been focused on the day-to-day struggles of living. Those factory workers, ranch hands, cowboys, drifters, miners, secretaries and waitresses, all ordinary folk forged and fashioned by hard places and rough times, served to inform our collective vision and overall tone for the movie.

Shooting ended in August 2004, and we moved on through postproduction. I saw rough cuts of the film, wrote detailed notes to the director and editor, listened to music cues, watched proposed trailers, viewed poster suggestions, voiced my opinions when necessary. A year later, Larry and I gathered together a group of close friends and family and headed to the Loft Theatre in Tucson for a private screening of *Brokeback Mountain*. I was scared. I had wanted this so badly for so long, and I wanted it all to work—not just for me, but for everyone who had worked on the film, and for Larry, for Annie. I set aside everything I'd experienced since production began, wanted to see it all with a fresh eye, and hunkered down to watch a movie.

Seeing our film in finished form up on the big screen was a kind of out-of-body experience. In spite of what I already knew about *Brokeback Mountain,* I was not at all prepared for the emotional tidal wave that swept over me: there I sat, having lived with these characters for over eight years—they had been more real to me at times than the corporeal—and I felt as if I were being introduced to them for the first time. After the credits rolled and the lights came up, everyone just sat there. The women were crying; the men were silent. No one spoke until we wandered outside.

*Brokeback Mountain* is an excellent movie, raw, spare, severe. It is a true collaboration, in every sense. I could write in detail about the specifics of the visual narrative and how they affected me, but watching the film was such a visceral experience that my words simply cannot do it justice. It is all of a piece now, and something everyone must discover for themselves.

The years of struggle, the rejections, the hard work, the fear and the monumental risk have all been worth it: *Brokeback Mountain* the film stands faithfully beside "Brokeback Mountain" the short story.

# Cast and Crew Credits

Focus Features and
River Road Entertainment Present

An Ang Lee Film

Heath Ledger

Jake Gyllenhaal

BROKEBACK MOUNTAIN

Linda Cardellini

Anna Faris

Anne Hathaway

Michelle Williams

and
Randy Quaid

Casting by
Avy Kaufman, CSA

Costume Designer
Marit Allen

Music Supervisor
Kathy Nelson

Music by
Gustavo Santaolalla

Edited by
Geraldine Peroni
Dylan Tichenor, ACE

Production Designer
Judy Becker

Director of Photography
Rodrigo Prieto, ASC, AMC

Co-Producer
Scott Ferguson

Executive Producers
William Pohlad
Larry McMurtry
Michael Costigan
Michael Hausman
Alberta Film Entertainment

Producers
Diana Ossana & James Schamus

Based on the Short Story by
Annie Proulx

Screenplay by
Larry McMurtry & Diana Ossana

Directed by
Ang Lee

Unit Production Managers
Scott Ferguson
Tom Benz

First Assistant Directors
Michael Hausman
Pierre Tremblay

**Cast**
(in order of appearance)

| | |
|---|---|
| Ennis del Mar | Heath Ledger |
| Jack Twist | Jake Gyllenhaal |
| Joe Aguirre | Randy Quaid |
| Waitress | Valerie Planche |
| Basque | David Trimble |
| Chilean Sheepherder #1 | Victor Reyes |
| Chilean Sheepherder #2 | Lachlan Mackintosh |
| Alma | Michelle Williams |
| Jolly Minister | Larry Reese |
| Timmy | Marty Antonini |
| Rodeo Clown | Tom Carey |
| Bartender #1 | Dan McDougall |

| | |
|---|---|
| Biker #1 | Don Bland |
| Biker #2 | Steven Cree Molison |
| Lureen Newsome | Anne Hathaway |
| Announcer | Duval Lang |
| Bartender #2 | Dean Barrett |
| Alma Jr., age 3 | Hannah Stewart |
| Monroe | Scott Michael Campbell |
| Fayette Newsome | Mary Liboiron |
| L. D. Newsome | Graham Beckel |
| Ennis, age 9 | Kade Philps |
| K. E. del Mar, age 11 | Steffen Cole Moser |
| Jenny, age 4 | Brooklyn Proulx |
| Alma Jr., age 5 | Keanna Dubé |
| Farmer #1 | James Baker |
| Farmer #2 | Pete Seadon |
| Alma Jr., age 9–12 | Sarah Hyslop |
| Jenny, age 7–8 | Jacey Kenny |
| Judge | Jerry Callaghan |
| Jenny, age 11 | Cayla Wolever |
| Alma Jr., age 13 | Cheyenne Hill |
| Bobby, age 10 | Jake Church |
| Roughneck #1 | Ken Zilka |
| Roughneck #2 | John Tench |
| Cassie | Linda Cardellini |
| Lashawn Malone | Anna Faris |
| Randall Malone | David Harbour |
| Alma Jr., age 19 | Kate Mara |
| Carl | Will Martin |
| Killer Mechanic | Gary Lauder |
| Grease Monkey | Christian Fraser |
| Assailant | Cam Sutherland |
| Jack's Mother | Roberta Maxwell |
| John Twist | Peter McRobbie |

**Stunts**

| | |
|---|---|
| Stunt Coordinator | Kirk Jarrett |
| | |
| Ennis Stunt Doubles | Dwayne Wiley |
| | Greg Schlosser |
| | Christian Fraser |
| | Tyler Thompson |
| Jack Stunt Doubles | Shane Pollitt |
| | Greg Schlosser |
| | Quentin Lowry |
| | Jody Turner |
| Lureen Stunt Double | Skyler Mantler |
| Joe Stunt Double | Ken Zilka |
| | |
| Driver | Guy Bews |
| Barrel Racer | Chyanne Hodgson |
| Bull Fighter #1 | Dave Leader |

| | |
|---|---|
| Bull Fighter #2 | Jory Vine |
| Bull Fighter #3 | Mark van Tienhoven |
| Bull Rider #1 | Greg Schlosser |
| Bull Rider #2 | Dwayne Wiley |
| Bull Dogger #1 | Shane Pollitt |
| Rodeo Hazers | T. J. Bews |
| | Lynn Ivall |
| | |
| Art Directors | Tracey Baryski |
| | Laura Ballinger |
| Assistant Art Director | Tori James |
| Set Decorators | Patricia Cuccia |
| | Catherine Davis |
| Alberta Match Set Decorators | Carrie Marklinger |
| | Loraine Edwards |
| Art Department Trainee | Ricardo Olinger |
| Graphic Artist | Pat Goettler |
| Draftsperson | Corrie Neyrinck |
| | |
| Second Unit DOP/B-Camera Operator | Peter Wunstorf |
| A-Camera/Steadicam Operator | Damon Moreau |
| First Assistant A-Camera | Trevor Holbrook |
| Second Assistant A-Camera | Garth Longmore |
| First Assistant B-Camera | Kirk Chiswell |
| Second Assistant B-Camera | Chris Bang |
| Camera Trainee | Kelly Strong |
| C-Camera Operator | Alic Chehade |
| First Assistant C-Camera | Chris Hassen |
| Second Assistant C-Camera | Brett Manyluk |
| Video Assist/Playback | Rob Doak |
| | |
| Script Supervisor | Karen Bedard |
| | |
| Production Sound Mixer | Drew Kunin |
| Boom Operator | Peter Melnychuk |
| Second Boom | Geo Major |
| | |
| Assistant Costume Designer | Renée Bravener |
| Costume Supervisors | Kelly Fraser |
| | Christine Thomson |
| Set Costume Supervisor | Jeffrey Fayle |
| Truck Costumer Supervisor | Devora Brown |
| Extras Costumer | Leslie Tufts |
| Pattern Cutter | Quynh Chestnut |
| Breakdown Artist | Lizzie McGovern |
| | Susan Montalbetti |
| Costumer | Katalin Berta |
| | |
| Department Head, Makeup | Manlio Rocchetti |
| Key Makeup Artist | Linda Melazzo |
| Department Head, Hair | Mary Lou Green |
| Key Hair | Penny Lea Thompson |

| | |
|---|---|
| Gaffers | Christopher Porter |
| | Chris Sprague |
| Best Boy Electric | David Vernerey |
| Genny Operator | Tony Skaper |
| Lamp Operators | Dean Merrells |
| | Landin Walsh |
| Lamp Operator Trainee | Colin Allen |
| Rigging Gaffer | Gordon Schmidt |
| Best Boy Rigging Electric | Al Whitmore |
| | |
| Key Grips | Kim Olsen |
| | John Adshead |
| Best Boy Grip | Alison Rigby |
| Dolly Grip | Tim Milligan |
| Key Rigging Grip | Ivan Hawkes |
| Grips | Corey Lee |
| | Chris Kosloski |
| Grip Trainee | Colin Fitzgerald |
| | |
| Property Master | Ken Wills |
| Assistant Property Master | Justin Onofriechuk |
| Props Buyer | Sherrie Wills |
| Props Trainee | Cory Wills |
| | |
| Special Effects Coordinator | Maurice Routly |
| Assistant Special Effects Coordinator | Jason Paradis |
| | |
| Production Coordinator | Hudson Cooley |
| First Assistant Production Coordinator | Marla Touw |
| Second Assistant Production Coordinator | Catherine McGovern |
| | |
| Second Assistant Director | Brad Moerke |
| Third Assistant Director | Kathy Ringer |
| Trainee Assistant Director | Travis McConnell |
| | |
| Assistant to Mr. Lee | Karen Redford |
| Assistant to Mr. Lee New York | David Lee |
| Assistant to Mr. Ledger | Neil Bell |
| Assistant to Mr. Gyllenhaal | Liat Baruch |
| Assistants to Mr. Schamus | Paul Getto |
| | Dave Targan |
| | Anikah McLaren |
| Assistant to Producers | Mathew Provost |
| Office Production Assistant | Steven Hanulik |
| Mr. Lee's Intern | Catherine Shao |
| Production Intern | Kurt Enger |
| Art Department Intern | Sara Ossana |
| Paint Intern | Colt Hausman |
| | |
| Dialect Coach | Joy Ellison |
| | |
| Lead Dresser | Tom Edwards |
| On Set Dressers | Chris Smith |
| | Jordy Wihak |

| | |
|---|---|
| Set Dresser | Chris MacRae |
| Set Buyer | Rene Jansen |
| Dressers | Leanna Thompson |
| | Mike Arzillo |
| | Rick Lovegrove |
| | Shane Nichol |
| | Jim Patrick |
| | |
| Stand-ins | Scott Urquhart |
| | Jamie Switch |
| | Meagen MacKenzie |
| | |
| Construction Coordinator | Jurgen Lutze |
| Construction Foreman | Gerald Gerlinsky |
| Construction Buyer | Otto Helmig |
| Head Carpenters | Dean Baker |
| | Larry Pollon |
| On Set Carpenter | Dana Rainer |
| Scenic Carpenters | Richard Brouillet |
| | Alain DuPerron |
| | Clair Hein |
| | Fred Norgard |
| Carpenters | Gabriel Bardwell |
| | Richard Barrett |
| | Michael Willis |
| | Katherine Young |
| Construction Labourer | Jesse Singleton |
| | |
| Scenic Paint Coordinator | Carol Anne Beiser-Haywood |
| Paint Foremen | Brad Kaughman |
| | Aaron McCullough |
| Sign Painters | Stuart Friesen |
| | Rick Janzen |
| On Set Painter | Charmaine Husum |
| Scenic Painters | BAarbara Chandler |
| | Christine MacDonald |
| | Loyola Lewis |
| | Larry Lucoe |
| Painters | Jessie Johnsen |
| | Jason Mackenzie |
| | Glen Tallis |
| | Jason Webster |
| | |
| Head Greensman | Thomas Yaremko |
| Lead Greens | Coral Tilbury-Dambrauskas |
| On Set Greens | Eugene Gogowich |
| | |
| Locations Manager | Darryl Solly |
| | |
| Assistant Locations Manager | Jay St. Louis |
| Trainee Locations Manager | Ed Huery |
| Locations Scouts | Charles May |
| | Cody Klepper |

| | |
|---|---|
| | Terry Marsh<br>Edssel Hilchie |
| Production Assistants | Sean Finnan<br>Dan Kuzmenko<br>Evan Godfrey<br>Cameron Dales<br>Tyler Flewelling<br>Mark Gamache<br>Naomi Robinson |
| Casting Associate | Elizabeth Greenberg |
| Canadian Casting | Deb Green, CDC |
| Canadian Casting Assistant | Erin Flasch |
| Vancouver Casting | Trish Robinson |
| Casting Assistant | Gloria Wright |
| Extras Casting | Alyson Lockwood |
| Additional Music by | Marcelo Zarvos |
| Post Production Supervisor | Gerry Robert Byrne |
| First Assistant Editors | Kimberly Saree Tomes<br>Shelby Siegel |
| Assistant Editor | Beth Moran |
| Post Production Assistants | Geoffrey Sledge<br>Kate Abernathy<br>Penny Sewell |
| Post Production Sound Facility | C5, Inc. |
| Supervising Sound Editors | Eugene Gearty<br>Philip Stockton |
| ADR Editor | Kenton Jakub |
| First Assistant Sound Editor | Igor Nikolic |
| FX Assistant Sound Editor | Larry Wineland |
| First Assistant Sound Editor | Chris Fielder |
| Sound Edit Intern | Sara Stern |
| Music Editors | Anibal Kerpel<br>Annette Kudrak |
| Foley Supervisor | Frank Kern |
| Foley Editor | Kam Chan |
| Foley Recordist/Engineer | George A. Lara |
| Foley Artist | Marko Costanzo |
| Foley Assistant | David Warzynski |
| ADR Mixers | Thomas J. O'Connell<br>Mike Fox |

| | |
|---|---|
| ADR Recordists | Rick Canelli<br>Mike Fox<br>Andy Wright<br>Jay Gallagher |
| ADR Recorded at | Warner Bros. Studio Facilities in Hollywood<br>Monkeyland Audio, Inc.<br>Soundfirm Sydney Pty. Ltd<br>Swelltone Labs |
| ADR Voice Casting | Barbara Harris |
| Re-Recording Mixers | Reilly Steele<br>Eugene Gearty |
| Re-Recordist | Terrance Laudermilch |
| Re-Recorded at | Sound One |
| Mix Technician | Avi Laniado |
| Insurance Provided by | AON / Albert G. Ruben |
| Legal Services provided by | Sheppard Mullin Richter & Hampton<br>Robert Darwell<br>Michael Holland |
| Music Legal and Clearances by | Christine Bergren<br>Jennifer Pray |
| Clearances by | Now Clear This Research<br>Jay Floyd<br>Michelle Dunta |
| Additional Clearances by | Searchworks, Inc.<br>Roxanne Mayweather<br>Suzanne Shelton |
| Production Accountant | Anne Hannan |
| Payroll Accountant | Jill Antal |
| Second Assistant Accountants | Patricia Compton<br>Robert Roscorla |
| Accounting Clerk | Val Brown |
| Post Production Accountant | Trevanna Post, Inc.<br>Jodi Yeager |
| Unit Publicist | David Linck |
| Still Photographer | Kimberley French |
| Transportation Coordinator | Dan Klepper |
| Transportation Captain | Tom Lloyd |

**Drivers**

| | |
|---|---|
| Kim Breckenridge | Eddie Washington |
| Dayle Simpson | Jody Hargraves |
| Dave McBean | Steven Shayler |

| | |
|---|---|
| Carla Klepper | Lawrence Gooch |
| Bruce Milward | Jacqueline Simpson |
| Frank Biro | Dave MacDonald |
| Darryl Bateman | Al Basaraba |
| Fred Dunphy | Debbie Porter |
| Mark Jones | Doss Griffiths |
| Coleman Robinson | Ralph McCoy |
| Ray Breckenridge | Alfie Creighton |
| Stew DePasse | |
| | |
| Animal Management | Gerry Hornbeck |
| | Wildlife Incorporated |
| Field Biologist | Martin Urquhardt |
| Animal Coordinator | TJ Bews |
| Animal Wrangler Captain | Ken Zilka |
| Dog Trainer | Florence Krisko |
| Assistant Dog Trainer | Cathy Vayda |
| Bear Trainer | Ruth LaFarge |
| Sheep Wrangler | Lachlan Mackintosh |
| Wranglers | Cam Sutherland |
| | Dwight Beard |
| | Dusty Bews |
| | Allen Bruisedhead |
| | Wright Bruisedhead |
| | Randy Dye |
| | Don Gillespie |
| | Clinton Holmes |
| | Alby King |
| | Dale Montgomery |
| | Shawn Wells |
| | |
| Catering | Cal-B-Ques |
| | Keith Church |
| Chef | Vance Wagner |
| Assistant Chefs | Ryan Chatfield |
| | Robert Demuth |
| Production Paramedic | Joan Armstrong |
| Paramedics | Gino Savoia |
| | Samantha Hughes |
| | Darren Grout |
| Craft Service | Chantal Teasdale |
| Assistant Craft Service | Dorothy Simpson |
| Security Coordinator | Peter Gurr |
| Extras Craft Service | Shirley Irvine |
| | Marty Arthur |

Visual Effects by Buzz Image Group Inc.

| | |
|---|---|
| Visual Effects Supervisor | Louis Morin |
| | |
| Senior Inferno Artist | François Métivier |
| Inferno Artist | Ara Khanikian |

| | |
|---|---|
| 3D Artists | Pierre-Simon Lebrun-Chaput |
| | François Lord |
| | Alexandre Lafortune |
| | Matthew Rouleau |
| | Philippe Sylvain |
| | Robin Tremblay |
| | Bruno-Olivier Laflamme |
| | Jean-François Lafleur |
| | |
| Roto Artists | Glenn Silver |
| | Marie-Josée Ouellet |
| Visual Effects Line Producer | Annie Godin |
| Visual Effects Production Secretary | Catherine Coley |
| | |
| Digital Opticals | Cine-byte Imaging Inc. |
| | |
| Senior Production Supervisors | Alan Bak |
| | Tom Bak |
| Production Supervisor | Rick Hannigan |
| Technical Supervisor | Jeff Baker |
| Digital Opticals/Titles | Mark Tureski |
| | Chris Ross |
| Scanning and Recording | Drake Conrad |
| | Felix Heeb |
| | Paul Mantler |
| | Jason Giberson |
| Production Coordinator | Diana Madureira |
| | |
| Title Design | yU + Co |
| | |
| Negative Cutter | Exact Cut |
| | Tom Mayclim |
| Prints by | Deluxe Toronto |
| Color Timer | Chris Hinton |
| Avid Equipment provided by | Pivotal Post |
| Dolby Sound Consultant | Brad Hohle |
| Continuity Dialogue Spotting List | Oncore Productions |
| | |
| Music Scoring Mixer | Anibal Kerpel |
| Orchestrations/Conductor | Richard Emerson |
| Strings Arranged by | David Campbell |
| Contractor | David Sabee |
| | |
| Score Produced by | Gustavo Santaolalla |
| Assistants to Mr. Santaolalla and Mr. Kerpel | Lucia Peraza |
| | Adrian Sosa |

## Songs

**The Cowboy's Lament**
Traditional

**Water Walking Jesus**
Written by
James McMurtry, Stephen Bruton and Annie Proulx

**Jukebox**
Written and Performed by
Ken Strange, Randall Pugh, and Ron Guffnett
Courtesy of Sourcerer

**Trust in Lies**
Written by Rick Garcia and Craig Eastman
Performed by The Raven Shadows featuring Tim Ferguson

**Battle Hymn of the Republic**
Traditional
Performed by Casey Smith, Darrell Croft,
Lloyd Pollock, Peter Orr, and Ken Hart

**I Won't Let You Go**
Written, Produced and Performed by
Gustavo Santaolalla

**No One's Gonna Love You Like Me**
Written and Produced by Gustavo Santaolalla
Performed by Mary McBride

**All Night Blues**
Written by Rick Garcia and Craig Eastman
Performed by The Raven Shadows

**I Love Doing Texas with You**
Written by Tom Wesselmann
Performed by Kevin Trainor
Courtesy of ACM Records

**King of the Road**
Written by Roger Miller
Performed by Roger Miller
Courtesy of Tree Productions

**A Love That Will Never Grow Old**
Written by Gustavo Santaolalla and Bernie Taupin
Performed by Emmylou Harris
Emmylou Harris appears courtesy of Nonesuch Records

**Quizas, Quizas, Quizas**
Written by Osvaldo Farres
Produced by Gustavo Santaolalla
Performed by Rick Garcia

**Capriccio Espagnol Op. 34**
Composed by Nikolaj Rimsky-Korsakov
Arranged by Jim Long

Performed by Philharmonia Slavonica
Courtesy of Point Classics LLC

**Mason Dixon Line**
Written by Jeff Wilson
Performed by Jeff Wilson
Courtesy of Marc Ferrari/Mastersource

**Devil's Right Hand**
Written by Steve Earle
Performed by Steve Earle

**It's So Easy**
Written by Buddy Holly
Performed by Linda Ronstadt
Courtesy of Elektra Entertainment Group
By arrangement with Warner Strategic Marketing

**Angel Went Up in Flames**
Written, Produced and Performed by
Gustavo Santaolalla

**I Don't Want to Say Goodbye**
Written and Produced by Gustavo Santaolalla
Performed by Teddy Thompson
Teddy Thompson appears courtesy of Verve Forecast

**D-I-V-O-R-C-E**
Written by Bobby Braddock and Curly Putman
Performed by Tammy Wynette
Courtesy of Epic Records
By arrangement with Sony BMG Music

**Melissa**
Written by Stephen Alaimo and Gregg Allman
Performed by The Allman Brothers
Courtesy of Island Def Jam Music Group
Under license from Universal Music Enterprises

**I'll Be Gone**
Written and Performed by
Terry Gadsden and Fred Kinck-Petersen
Courtesy of DeWolfe Music

**I'm Always on a Mountain When I Fall**
Written by Merle Haggard
Performed by Merle Haggard
Courtesy of Tree Productions

**Eyes of Green**
Written by Jeff Wilson
Performed by Jeff Wilson
Courtesy of Marc Ferrari/Mastersource